What the critics are saying:

"I absolutely inhaled this book! I read this book twice in one sitting. I read it so fast the first time…, I then had to read it again immediately, at a slower pace…If you like the writing styles of Fiona Brand, Suzanne Brockman, Shannon McKenna, Cindy Dees or Linda Howard, then you should not miss this book by Lisa Marie Rice" – *Tressa Harvey, Sensual Romance*

"Midnight Man is a roller coaster ride of emotion. Be warned to keep tissues and a glass of ice water handy. You'll be biting your nails with anxiety one minute and squirming in your chair to find relief the next." – *Oleta M Blaylock, Just Erotic Romance Reviews*

"Lisa Marie Rice tells a wonderful tale of love and intrigue in the MIDNIGHT MAN…Lisa Marie Rice's stunning debut and an author to keep an eye out for in the future" – *Lisa Lambrect, In The Library Reviews*

"Like a sinful and satisfying addiction, you'll need every bit of willpower to put this story down. MIDNIGHT MAN ranks right up there with decadent chocolate: a touch of sweet, a bite of dark, and mouthwateringly good until it's all eaten up. A whirlwind attraction mingled into a suspenseful adventure, MIDNIGHT MAN is a steamy romance story guaranteed to be a favorite." – *Serena Thatcher, The Word On Romance*

"Sizzling sexual tension, raging passion and a menacing unknown danger all blend together to create a highly volatile and explosive story ..... For a story with plenty of sizzle, and characters who are exciting and likable, I highly recommend MIDNIGHT MAN." – *Terrie Figueroa, Romantic Suspense Reviews*

MIDNIGHT MAN

MIDNIGHT BOOK 1

by Lisa Marie Rice

MIDNIGHT MAN
An Ellora's Cave Publication, October 2004

Ellora's Cave Publishing, Inc.
1337 Commerce Drive, Suite 13
Stow OH 44224

ISBN #1-4199-5050-9

MS Reader (LIT) ISBN #1-84360-461-2
Other available formats (no ISBNs are assigned):
Adobe (PDF), Rocketbook (RB), Mobipocket (PRC) & HTML

Edited by *Marty Klopfenstein*
Cover art by *Syneca*

Warning:

The following material contains graphic sexual content meant for mature readers. ***Midnight Man*** has been rated E-rotic by a minimum of three independent reviewers.

Ellora's Cave Publishing offers three levels of Romantica™ reading entertainment: S (S-ensuous), E (E-rotic), and X (X-treme).

S-*ensuous* love scenes are explicit and leave nothing to the imagination.

E-*rotic* love scenes are explicit, leave nothing to the imagination, and are high in volume per the overall word count. In addition, some E-rated titles might contain fantasy material that some readers find objectionable, such as bondage, submission, same sex encounters, forced seductions, etc. E-rated titles are the most graphic titles we carry; it is common, for instance, for an author to use words such as "fucking", "cock", "pussy", etc., within their work of literature.

X-*treme* titles differ from E-rated titles only in plot premise and storyline execution. Unlike E-rated titles, stories designated with the letter X tend to contain controversial subject matter not for the faint of heart.

Also by Lisa Marie Rice:

Christmas Angel

Midnight Book 1: *Midnight Man*

Midnight Book 2: *Midnight Run*

Port of Paradise

Woman On the Run

MIDNIGHT MAN

MIDNIGHT BOOK 1

by Lisa Marie Rice

Chapter One

December 21st
Portland, Oregon

She's scared of me, he thought.

Damn right.

Seven hours ago, he'd killed two men and wounded four others. Death and violence clung to him like a shroud. He was still wired from the kill, blood pumping.

Which might be why ever since crossing the threshold of Suzanne Barron's office, he couldn't think of anything but bedding the damned woman.

John Huntington eyed Suzanne Barron across her very stylish desk in her very stylish office. She was stylish herself: classy, elegant, stunningly beautiful. Smooth, creamy ivory skin, dark honey-blonde hair, gray eyes like a pool of still mountain water, watching him warily.

"So, Mr. Huntington, you didn't say in your email exactly what your business is."

The way she was looking at him, if he'd said *'bear hunting and cannibalism'* she just might believe him.

In the corporate world he was a wolf carefully dressed in the sheep's clothing of pencil pushers—Brioni and Armani. It took a while to see the kind of man he was and some people never managed until it was too late.

But right now, just in from Venezuela, he looked like the wolf he was. In black leather jacket, black turtleneck sweater, black jeans and combat boots, adrenaline still coursing through his system, he wasn't anyone pretty Ms. Barron would or should want in her building. Especially since—he'd seen the signs—she lived alone.

She was already leery of him and she didn't even know about the Sig-Sauer in the shoulder holster, the K-bar knife in the scabbard between his shoulder blades or the .22 in the ankle holster, otherwise she would have probably ordered him out of the building.

She watched him, anxiety clouding luminous eyes.

He was coming down off an adrenaline high. The consulting job teaching soft oil executives in Venezuela how to deal with a hard world had gone very bad very fast. A small army of Frente de la Libertad terrorists had come down from the hills and tried to kidnap the entire top management of Western Oil Corporation there on a junket.

Luckily he'd been on the spot and had routed them, taking down two tangos and wounding four. The rest had been mopped up by the local police.

John had been flown back up Stateside in the grateful CEO's private Learjet, with a contract to provide security for Western Oil worldwide until the end of time and a $300,000 bonus check in his pocket, just in time for his appointment with the gorgeous Ms. Suzanne Barron.

Time to convince her that he wasn't dangerous. He was, but not to her.

"I own and run my own company, Alpha Security International, Ms. Barron. I have an office just off Pioneer Square, but my company is expanding quickly and I need new premises. There's plenty of space here."

John looked around her office. He hadn't been expecting anything like this. The ad in *The Oregonian* had simply stated the footage and the location, in Pearl, a rough part of town slowly gentrifying. Outside was a wasteland. Walking through the front door of the two-story brick building had been like walking into a little slice of heaven.

And the four interconnected rooms she'd showed him—it was as if they'd been fashioned for him. Large, spacious, high ceilinged. The smell of new wood and old brick, so completely different from the modern crapola suite he'd rented in an expensive high rise off Pioneer Square.

Inside, the building felt like an exquisite jewel with its brass fittings, light hardwood floors and soft pastel furniture. She'd put up some discreet lights to mark the holiday season and the air was spiced with the evergreen boughs on the heavy mantelpiece and what smelled like oranges and cinnamon.

Harp music that sounded as if it was being beamed down directly from heaven played softly from hidden speakers.

He'd had an instant sense of homecoming, strange in a man who'd never had a home. His nerves, still jangled from the takedown, started calming. This was exactly what he'd been looking for, without knowing he was looking for it.

Add to that the cool, luscious blonde who'd met him at the door, offering her soft, slim hand. His body, already primed for battle, had immediately become primed for sex.

Hell, since when had he become so easily distractible? In the normal course of events, gunfire couldn't distract him from a mission. Of course, gunfire wasn't a wildly attractive blonde, but his mission here was to find a new office and now that he'd seen this place, he was determined to have it. And the landlady. But first, he had to get his hormones under control; otherwise he'd come up empty-handed on both counts.

Down boy, he ordered himself.

He must be pumping hormones into the air by the ton, because she was sitting way back in her chair in an unconscious attempt to put distance between them—the thought that a desk and some air could stop him if he really wanted to jump her was so ludicrous he wanted to snort—and her eyes were so wide he could see the milky whites around the pupils.

Time to get her to climb down from that emotional ledge and reassure her that he wouldn't gobble her up.

Not yet anyway.

He studied the room, deliberately not looking at her. He kept his face bland, giving her time to study him, and heard her breathing start to slow down.

Pretending to study the room was a ploy but he soon found himself distracted by its beauty. He didn't have the tools to analyze how she did it, but he could appreciate the end result. Stunning, soft pastel colors. Comfortable furniture that managed to be both modern and feminine. She'd kept the architectural details of the period—early '20s he'd guess. Everything—every detail, every nook and cranny, every object—was gorgeous.

She'd had enough time to calm down so he turned back to her.

"Did you do the restoration work, Ms. Barron?"

The question relaxed her. She looked around, a smile curving soft pale pink lips. It was raining outside. The dim water-washed light coming in through the tall windows turned her skin the color of the mother of pearl bowl holding some kind of fragrant plant on the windowsill.

"Yes. I inherited the building from my grandparents. It used to be a shoe factory but the company went bankrupt 20 years ago and has stood empty ever since. I'm a designer and I decided to restore it myself instead of selling it."

"You did a wonderful job."

Her eyes rose to meet his. She stared at him and her breath came out in a little huff. "Thank you."

She toyed for a moment with a pen, tapping it lightly against the highly polished surface of the desk. Realizing she was betraying nerves, she put it down again. Her hands were as lovely as the rest of her, slim and white. She had two expensive-looking rings on her right hand, no rings on the left.

Good. No other man had her and now that he'd spotted her, no other man was going to get her. Not until he'd finished with her and that was going to take a long, long time.

Her hands were trembling slightly.

Suzanne Barron might be one of the loveliest women he'd ever seen but reduced to essentials she was an animal—a human animal—and she could sense, probably smell, the danger in him, especially acute now.

He'd always had this effect on civilians. Well, he reminded himself, he was a civilian now, too. He wasn't in the service anymore where he could be instantly recognized for what he was.

All his life he'd lived in a fraternity of like-minded men, friend or foe. Fellow warriors knew who he was and usually treaded lightly around him.

Civilians never knew how to cope, like lambs sensing a tiger had infiltrated the flock. Uneasy without knowing why.

Moving slowly so as not to alarm her, he reached across and handed her a folder. His hand briefly touched hers. It was like touching silk. Gray eyes widened at the touch and he withdrew.

She rested her hand on the cover sheet. A small furrow developed between curved ash eyebrows.

"What's this, Mr. Huntington?"

"References, Ms. Barron. My CV, service record, credit rating from my bank, three letters of recommendation, and a list of the major clients of my company." He smiled. "I'm honest, pay my taxes, I'm solvent and practice good hygiene."

"I don't doubt any of that, Mr. Huntington."

A thin line appeared between her brows as she leafed through the folder. He kept still, moving only his lungs, a trick he'd learned on the battlefield.

"What do you mean by service—Oh." She looked up. Something moved in her eyes. "You're a Commander. An officer in the Army." He could see her relaxing faintly. An officer seemed safe to her. She couldn't know what he'd done in the service; otherwise she sure as hell wouldn't be relaxing.

"*Was* an officer. My discharge papers are in there, too. And I was in the Navy." He tried to keep the scorn out of his voice and barely restrained himself from snorting. Army indeed. Candy-ass soldiers, all of them. "It's not the same thing."

Her smile deepened. She was softening. Good. John was good at reading body language. The lease was a done deal. She relaxed as she read his service record.

The record mentioned some of his medals, enough to impress a civilian. The rest—for missions no one would ever know about—were in his shadowbox.

The list of clients didn't hurt, either. He had more than a few Fortune 500 companies in there.

She now knew he wasn't going to get drunk and disorderly. He wasn't going to skip town without paying the rent. He wasn't going to make off with her silver. Which was something, since she had a lot of it in here, mostly in the form of antique silver frames and a collection of tea services. Everything in his file said he was a sober highly respected citizen.

What the file didn't mention was that before becoming an officer he'd been a trained sniper-scout, with a certified kill at 1,500 yards. That he knew 45 different ways of killing a man with his bare hands. That he could blow up her building with what was under her kitchen sink, and that by this time tomorrow night he'd be in her bed, in her.

"Navy. Navy officer. Sorry. Should I call you Commander Huntington or Mister Huntington?"

"John would do nicely, ma'am. I'm retired."

"John. I'm Suzanne." A lull in the rain outside created a little oasis of quiet in the room.

All his senses were keen. He could hear the breath going in and out of her lungs, the slick sound of nylon as she recrossed her legs under the desk.

He had a view only of the delicate ankles but he knew they were attached to long, slender legs. He could just feel her thighs around his waist, calves hugging his hips…

"I beg your pardon?" She'd said something and he'd been so busy fantasizing getting her into bed he'd missed it.

John shifted, uncomfortably aware that it had been over six months since he'd last had sex. He'd just been too damned busy with getting his company up and running. Their gazes met and held.

"You'll want to call the people on that list." He kept his voice low, calm, unthreatening.

"I will, yes." She drew in a deep breath. "Well, um..." She turned a ring nervously around her finger. "So. I guess—I guess you'll be my new tenant. My first. You can do whatever you want in the rental. Though I'd rather you didn't knock down any walls."

"I could never in a million years do as good a job as you did decorating your office. I might just hire you to do mine."

"Actually, um..." Her pale skin turned the most delicate, delightful pink. She reached behind her for a file. She opened it and turned it around so he could see it. "While designing this office, I fiddled with a few ideas for the rental. I used a different color scheme, made it more..." She looked up at him through thick lashes—"more masculine." John moved his chair forward. His senses were so heightened that he could smell her skin. Some mixture of lotion and perfume and warm woman. She was blushing furiously now under his intense scrutiny.

John wrenched his gaze back to the drawings she had fanned out on the desktop, and then he focused in on what he was seeing.

Amazing.

"This is wonderful," he breathed. He studied each sheet carefully. She'd used unusual tones—dark gray and cream and a funny blue—to create a sleek, modern environment. Practical, comfortable, refined. It was as if she had walked around inside his head to pull out exactly what he wanted without him knowing he wanted it. "Elegant, but understated. I really like the beige ceiling with the blue thingies."

"Ecru." She smiled.

"I beg your pardon?"

"I'm sure you have technical terms in your business, Commander Huntington—John. Just as I have them in mine. The colors are slate, ecru and teal, not gray, beige and blue. And the blue thingies are stencils." She pushed the drawings across the desk to him. "Keep these. You're welcome to them. And if you need any help in getting the furnishings, let me know. Nothing in my design is custom-made. You could buy everything immediately. I'd be happy to help. I get a professional discount at all the major retailers."

"That's very generous of you. Would you be willing to design living quarters for me, too? For a fee, of course."

She drew in a quick breath. "Living quarters? You want—you want to live here, too?"

"Mm. There's plenty of space. Those three big back rooms would be more than enough for me. I keep odd hours in my business and I need to be close to the office. This would suit me fine. Now I want you to call some of the people on the list on page two."

"I beg your pardon?" When she shifted in her chair, some floral scent wafted his way. His nostrils flared to take it in.

"I've provided five people as character references. Call them. Call them before we sign the lease. We can do that tomorrow."

"I'm sure that won't be necessary, Comm—John."

"It's absolutely necessary, Suzanne." He looked around then brought his gaze back to her. "This is a beautiful space and you've done a great job renovating the building, but we're in a rough neighborhood."

It was one of the reasons he wanted his corporate headquarters here. He sometimes hired people who had looked wildly out of place in the prissy downtown building. Like Jacko, with his pierced nostrils and the viper tats.

"If you're going to be alone in a building with a man, you need to know who he is and that you're safe with him." His eyes bored into hers. "You'll be safe with me."

But not from me, he thought.

"I guess you're the expert." She blew out a little breath.

"Yes, ma'am. You'll call?"

Her eyes dropped to the paper. "Of course, if you want me to. You have an impressive list of references. Wait. Lieutenant Tyler Morrison, Portland Police Department. You know him?"

"Bud? Sure. We were in the service together. Then he quit and became a cop. Call him. And one more thing before I sign. What's your security system?"

"Security system? You mean like the alarm system? Let me check." She opened a Filofax and started poring over the pages with a tapered, pink-tipped finger. "I don't remember off-hand, but I know it was expensive. Ah, here we are. Interloc. Do you know them? Oh, how stupid of me. Of course you do, security is your business."

"I deal in personal security, not building security, but I know them." Interloc was a crappy outfit. They'd have snowed her with fancy alarms and 7 digit codes and their equipment could have come out of a cereal box. No freakin' way was he going to live and work in a building secured by Interloc. He stood up. "I'd appreciate it if you were to secure the alarms after I leave."

"I—okay." She stood up too, looking puzzled, and walked around the desk. "If you really want me to. I tend to just have the door locked during the day because it's so fussy putting on the alarm system then switching it off when I want to go out. So...I guess we have a deal?"

"You bet."

He stuck out his hand. After a second's hesitation, she offered hers. It was almost half the size of his, slim and fine-boned. He carefully applied a little pressure and ordered himself to let go. It was damned hard to do. What he wanted to do was pull her into his arms and take her down to the floor.

Some of that must have been coming through because her eyes widened in alarm. He stepped back.

"I'll start moving my stuff in tomorrow. And I'll definitely be taking you up on your offer to help me decorate. Of course I'd like to pay for the design of my office. I can see that a lot of work went into it."

She waved that away. "No, don't worry. I was just doodling. Consider the design a welcome present." She turned into the hallway and he followed, trying not to ogle her backside and trying not to be obvious about smelling the air in her wake. His men said he had the sense of smell of a bloodhound. He could smell cigarette smoke on a man's clothes a day after he'd smoked. Suzanne Barron's smell nearly brought him to his knees.

Her scent was perfume, something light and floral, mixed in with an apple-scented shampoo, the smell of freshly washed clothing and some indefinable something that he just knew was her skin. Soon, very soon, he'd be smelling her skin close up. Just a matter of time.

The sooner the better. Christ, the view from the back was as enticing as the one from the front—sleek curves, dark-honey hair bouncing with every step she took.

He'd never seen a woman as curvy yet as delicately made as Suzanne Barron. Everything about her was dainty, fine-boned. He was going to have to be careful. No rough sex when he took her to bed. He'd have to enter her slowly, let her get used to him before…

She turned and smiled at him. "That's all right, then."

All right! His eyes narrowed and his body quickened until he stopped himself just short of reaching for her. She's talking about the lease, you idiot, he told himself.

"I'll get a contract drawn up and have a copy of the keys made for you. When do you want to start moving in?"

Now! His body clamored. Right this second. But he had things to take care of. "I don't have much to move. Mostly filing cabinets and computer equipment. Lots of that." He smiled into her eyes. "You're going to order the rest of the furnishings for me, right? Spend whatever you have to, I'll be good for it."

She was looking up at him, breathing slowly.

"Right, Suzanne?"

She blinked and seemed to come out of a daze. "Oh, yes, um, that's right. And I'll have a copy of the keys made for you."

He opened the door. The contrast between what was behind him—a delicate lady in a jewel of a building—and what was in front of him—bleak burned out storefronts, liquor stores and empty lots—made him turn back to her. Little Miss Muffet had to know that there were spiders out there. Big bad ones.

"Check me out, Suzanne. Make sure you know whom you're putting in your house. Call Bud. Call him now."

Pale pink lips slightly parted, gray eyes wide, she stared at him. "Okay, I..." She swallowed. "I will."

"And set the security system when I leave."

She nodded, her eyes never leaving his face.

"Do you know the seven digit code by heart?"

"How do you—? All right, no I don't."

"Start getting used to keeping the building secure. Learn the code by heart. I'll bet you keep the code on a piece of paper taped to the underside of your desk. You're right-handed so it's probably taped to the right side."

She blew out a little breath and nodded. Bingo.

"That's not good. From now on keep the code in a safe and memorize it. You've got a security system, so use it. I want this building locked down after I leave."

"Yessir, Commander, sir." A dimple twinkled then disappeared. "Or would that be aye aye?"

"The correct answer is—yes, I'll do exactly as you say."

She was so close he could have seen the pores in her skin if she'd had any. Instead, her skin was as smooth and perfect as marble, except soft and warm, he'd bet. He had one foot out the door, stepping from one world into another. He had to force himself to move.

"Lock the door, Suzanne," he said again as he crossed the threshold, pulling on the handle.

He waited patiently on the steps until he heard the distinctive whump-ding of the Interloc security alarm going on then walked down the steps into the rainy morning.

Chapter Two

Whew.

Suzanne leaned against her door and put a trembling fist to her racing heart. Her legs felt like wax and she wanted to slide down to the floor in a puddle.

John Huntington—*Commander* John Huntington—wasn't anything like what she'd been expecting.

The email had been innocent enough: Dear Ms. Barron, Saw your ad in *The Oregonian* today for the lease of office space and am interested in viewing the premises. I am looking for corporate headquarters for my company. If it would suit you, I would like to make an appointment for 10 a.m. on the 21st of December. John Huntington, President, ASI.

How nice. A CEO, she'd thought as she emailed back. An image of a white-haired avuncular type floated in her mind. A businessman. Perfect.

Pearl was gentrifying at a dizzy pace, but pockets of it were still very dangerous. Having a businessman around would make her feel safe.

The one thing the man sitting across from her didn't make her feel was safe. Scared, maybe. No, not scared, really, just…what?

Not a white haired fatherly type at all. Not old. Not safe. He looked dangerous. That was it. That was what had Suzanne's entire system on alert.

At first she thought the wrong man had come. He hadn't looked like the president of a company. He looked rough, dangerous. Like a biker, not a businessman. A big man, shoulders so broad they spanned the chair back, black, close-cropped hair with a dusting of silver at the temples, eyes somewhere between a very dark blue and brown, impossible to guess at in the uncertain watery light.

Whatever the color, though, he'd looked at her as if he were about to swallow her up whole.

She'd never seen a man so blatantly…male. Of course, she thought, with a wry shake of her head, the men she met as a decorator were a little different from the men in the Navy. Still, the brute male power he'd exuded had been overwhelming.

He hadn't done anything, had barely moved in his chair, never fidgeting or moving position, he hadn't said or done anything untoward, but she'd felt her entire body go into overdrive. She'd kept her hands from trembling only by sheer force of will.

This was crazy and had to stop now. John Huntington was paying a lot of money for the rental—more money, actually, than it was worth, given the location. So she was going to have to start getting used to him as a tenant. She couldn't afford to have to stand against a door and wait for her heart rate to slow down every time she saw him.

Maybe I should get out more, she thought. Stop working so hard. Start dating. Get a life.

Maybe the next time her bank manager asked her out, she should accept, instead of making an excuse. They'd dated a few times. Except Marcus Freeman was so pale, even by Portland white bread standards, and so boring. His hands were soft and white. Not broad and dark and hard like John Huntington's hands…

Stop that!

Good Lord, what was the matter with her?

Feeling her legs steady now beneath her, and able to bear her weight, she walked back down the hallway to her office. Seeing the familiar objects, each one hand-picked, each one with a history, calmed her. She'd had such pleasure designing this place, with the hardwood floors, beveled stained glass windows and terracotta sconces. The color and shapes gave her a lift, brightened her day.

Odd how her design for the rental unit was so completely different.

One rainy afternoon, when she had nothing better to do, she had walked across the hallway into the part of the building she wanted to rent out. Four rooms, one after another. The spaces were big and empty, a blank canvas.

Designing always excited her and she was usually quick, but that day, as she sat cross-legged on the big, empty hardwood floor, back against the wall, the design had just come pouring out of her, as if she were sketching a vision already formed. As if she already knew something darkly powerful were coming.

Her own office and living quarters were colorful and feminine. But the rental had come flowing out from her hand in shades of slate and ecru and teal, sleek and streamlined. It was as if she'd had John Huntington in mind as she'd sketched, had sensed his power and strength.

She'd seen the look of recognition in his eyes and knew that somehow she'd designed something that fit him.

Somehow she'd known that he'd need an oversized armchair, in soft black leather. Somehow she'd known that a man like him wouldn't like fuss or objects d'art—just a long linear desk made of titanium and black marble, open faced bookshelves, a teal and cream Chinese rug in geometric patterns.

For his bedroom, she'd choose an oversized bed with a mahogany headboard. An image of John Huntington in bed, naked, made her thighs suddenly tremble and clench. His pectorals had been visible beneath the sweater. His chest was probably covered with thick black body hair, narrowing down to…

This was crazy. She was crazy.

Shaken, Suzanne sat down behind her desk and tried to focus on something other than John Huntington's body. Magnificent though it was…

Her hands clenched on the desk and she stared at her white knuckles for a long moment. Grabbing the cordless handset, she leafed through the phone book until she found the number she sought.

"Portland Police Department," a bored voice announced.

"Lieutenant Morrison, please."

A click and then another voice. "Homicide."

"I'd like to speak with Lieutenant Morrison."

"Hold."

There was a lot of background noise. Someone screamed, then she heard male voices shouting, the sounds of scuffling, then a deep voice came on the line. "Morrison. What?"

Suzanne smiled. Bud sounded harassed and out of breath. "Bud, this is Suzanne. I wonder—"

"Suzanne." His deep voice sharpened. "Hey, is something wrong? Has something happened to Claire?"

"No, no, it's nothing like that."

Bud was engaged to her best friend, Claire Parks. Suzanne had met him on a couple of social occasions. He was absolutely besotted with Claire, but she was beginning to have doubts. Too macho, too take-control, too protective, she'd said. Tall and tough looking, and a friend of John Huntington's to boot, Suzanne could see Claire's point.

"Claire's fine. No, I'm calling about something else. I'm calling because my new tenant put your name down as a reference."

"So you've finally found a tenant. Good. Claire's worried about you all alone in that part of town and, frankly, so am I. Who'd you rent it out to?"

"A man named John Huntington. Commander John Huntington, a former naval officer. Do you know him? "

"John?" He gave a short laugh. "I sure do. And if he's your new tenant, then your troubles are over, honey."

Or just beginning, she thought. "Can you tell me something about him? What's his history?"

"Well, he was a damned fine soldier. Got a chest full of medals."

"Yes, I saw that on his discharge sheet."

"Hon, that would only give the medals he won for overt operations. He's got a safe full of the other ones. The ones for operations we don't know anything about, and never will."

Other ones? "What—what kind of soldier was he?"

"A SEAL. Elite commando. Best of the best. Expert in black ops. Operated best under cover of darkness. His men called him the Midnight Man. Got superb night vision. Probably killed more tangos—that's terrorists—than you've had hot dinners. Ha-ha."

"Ha-ha," Suzanne echoed hollowly. She had no trouble at all believing what Bud was telling her. The stillness, the palpable aura of danger about the man, told its own story. She'd just let into her home a very dangerous man. Not a simple soldier at all, but a trained killer. A man who killed for his country, true, but a killer nonetheless.

Bud interrupted her thoughts. "Say, how come Midnight Man is renting from you? I didn't even know he was in town. I heard he retired on disability, but he disappeared from sight after that."

"Disability?" The man she'd seen hadn't looked disabled at all. The contrary, in fact. "He didn't strike me as disabled."

"He got shot up pretty bad about a year ago, busted his knee. Navy bought him a new one, but he can't operate at peak levels any more. I don't know what he's doing now."

"He has an international security company. Named Alpha Security."

"You don't say." Suzanne heard a low whistle. "Alpha Security's a classy company. Got a really good rep. So Alpha's John's, huh? He's living in Portland now?"

"Guess so."

"Well, I'll be damned. You tell that son of a—er, son of a gun that he'd better get in touch, pronto. And honey—don't worry about John. He's honest and totally, completely reliable—and if he's head of Alpha he's more than solvent. I'm glad he'll be in the building with you. Now we don't have to worry about you in Pearl. You've got a really dangerous guy on your side there." The background noise level rose again. Dear God, was that the sound of a shot?

"Morrison, get your ass over here pronto!" someone shouted.

"Hey Suzanne, gotta run, it's a real zoo here today. See you."

Really dangerous guy. Suzanne was standing beside her desk. She put the cordless back in the handset and stared blindly down at her hand. A really dangerous guy was going to live right across the hall from her.

But she wasn't supposed to worry about anything.

Right.

"So you did call Bud. Good," a deep, rough voice said and she screamed.

"Oh my God!" She reared back in shock.

He was standing right in front of her, even larger and taller than she remembered.

"Here." A flick of his big hand and a plastic card, a pair of small needle-nosed pliers and a bent steel rod fell on her desktop. "That's what it took to get through your security. Because I was in a hurry. Given a bit more time, I could have done it with spit and a wire. So that's what your security system is worth—hey!"

Her heart was pummeling its way out of her chest. She had to sit and there was nowhere to sit. Trying to move, she stumbled and was pulled against a massive chest as she tried to focus past the bright spots in front of her eyes.

"Hey, hey, calm down. Sorry I scared you. I just wanted to show you that you need to upgrade your security. Nothing like a live demonstration to convince people. You weren't supposed to faint on me."

She wasn't even listening to the words. His voice was a deep meaningless rumble in his chest. She rested her forehead against his collarbone, palms up over his pectorals.

He was holding her tightly, so tightly she could hear—even feel—his calm strong heartbeat, one beat to her two.

He'd been out in the rain. He smelled delicious—some heady mixture of male, rain and leather. She moved her right hand slightly under his jacket and felt a leather harness of some sort. Intrigued, she moved her hand further across his chest and encountered grained wood and a steel barrel.

He wasn't letting go. She was going breathless from another type of shock now. One big hand covered the back of her head, the other clasped her about the waist. He pressed hard with that hand and her stomach came into contact with something equally hard.

Not a gun.

She jumped back as if scalded. Some dim part of her brain realized that she was able to do that only because he'd opened his arms the instant he felt her jolt. Otherwise there was no way she could have freed herself from his embrace. The muscles she'd pushed against to jump back were like steel.

Wordless, she stared at him.

"You need a new security system," he said.

She opened her mouth but nothing came out. New security system. The words circled around her head but couldn't find a place to land. She couldn't get a handle on them, on her emotions.

His expression was completely unchanged. Set, unsmiling, serious. She couldn't begin to read his reaction.

If he even had one. He seemed completely unaffected. And yet she knew he had been affected in at least one big way.

Embarrassment was coming in right after the shock, in great rolling waves. She could feel the heat of it rise in her face, together with another heat, completely uncontrollable.

Suzanne searched in her depths for some way to deal with the situation. Some nice neutral ladylike etiquette that would help her handle having felt the penis of a complete stranger.

Erect penis, if you please.

Huge, erect penis.

Oh God.

Her gaze shot to about six inches above his head. Her throat was dry and her lungs hurt.

"You need a new security system," he repeated. New security system. New. Security. System. She needed a new security system.

Well…yes. If he was able to break through her system in the time it took her to place a phone call, she probably did need a new one.

"Okay," she croaked. She cleared her throat. "Okay. I'll look into it as soon as I can. I'll ask around—"

"Don't bother. I'll install one for you. One not even I can get through. As a thank you for your designs."

"You don't need to—" Suzanne looked at his face. Not a face you said no to. "Okay. Thanks."

"What's your favorite restaurant here in Portland?"

She huffed out a little breath, shifting gears. "Well, I suppose… Comme Chez Soi. But why do you—"

"We can talk about your new system tonight, over dinner." He stated it as a fact, like gravity.

"Dinner?"

He nodded. "I'll pick you up at seven."

Suzanne fumbled to get her bearings, but balance eluded her. She couldn't even begin to think, not with this man in the same room, sucking out all the oxygen and taking with it all her common sense.

She said the only thing she could say. "Okay."

"Bring a key for me because I won't be able to install the new security system until the day after tomorrow at the earliest. I'll be sleeping here tomorrow night. I'll bring my bed first thing."

Bed. His bed. Suzanne could imagine him only too well in his bed, big body sleeping in tangled sheets.

"Okay," she whispered.

He stared at her for another few seconds, dark eyes boring into hers as if he could walk inside her mind. Then he nodded and walked towards the door. He didn't seem to rush but he covered ground fast. In a second, he was out the door.

Large as he was, he didn't make any noise. How could that be? He was wearing boots and they had to make some sound on hardwood flooring, didn't they?

But he disappeared as silently as he had come. He'd appeared before her as suddenly as a ghost. And then he was gone.

Suzanne stared at where he'd been long after she heard the front door snick shut, then groped blindly for a chair. She had a busy day ahead of her but she couldn't go anywhere until her legs stopped trembling.

Chapter Three

At 1900 on the dot, John rang Suzanne's front doorbell and at 1901 he heard the light click of her heels on the floor inside. She was punctual; he had to say that for her.

John supposed he shouldn't be surprised. Suzanne Barron was a businesswoman, after all, and a successful one at that. You don't survive in business if you can't meet a schedule.

He'd found the business world, in its own way, as demanding as the Navy.

John stood patiently outside the door, refraining from picking her locks and cutting through the alarm system out of pity. He'd made his point.

No, he stood outside her ridiculous excuse for a door and rang the bell, like a normal human male waiting for a female. To go out. Out on a date.

He supposed that's how you do it. Man waits for woman outside door. His dating experience was pretty limited. Usually when he wanted sex he'd go to an off-base bar and cast his net until someone bit. Sometimes it took five minutes, sometimes ten.

The women weren't looking for hearts and flowers and he wasn't looking to give it to them.

Suzanne Barron was an entirely different matter. Getting into her bed was going to require some finesse and some dusting off of his rusty social skills. He was going to have to make some polite non-business-related conversation, something he rarely had with civilians.

Why couldn't he just fast forward to the good part? He shrugged his shoulders under the cashmere overcoat that was part of his businessman disguise, wishing they were already in bed, recognizing how unusual it was for him to be so impatient.

He'd once hidden behind a boulder in one of the nastier 'Stans for four days and four nights without moving a muscle to get a shot at one of Abdul Rasheem's lieutenants. This itchy feeling was unlike him.

He was going to have to get through this evening. And probably a few other evenings after this one. Asking her out to dinner—out on dates—was necessary. There had to be something between meeting her and having sex. He couldn't just say, 'Let's go to bed.' It didn't work that way, not with ladies.

Or so he presumed. He didn't have much experience with the species. So here he was, locked into getting through an evening making conversation.

He didn't want to make nice.

He didn't want to have to give his opinion on how to decorate his new office. He just wanted to dump the whole problem in those pretty hands of hers and let her take care of it. And he sure as hell didn't need her input into what security system the building needed. He was fine with that.

What he wanted was to skip dinner and go straight to bed. Feel those long, slender legs wrapped around his waist. Sink into her. She'd be hot and tight…

He sighed and shifted, jaws clenched. It was altogether likely that getting into her building was easier than getting into her bed.

The door swung open and there she was, Suzanne Barron, as of this morning his new landlady and just about the most desirable woman he'd ever seen, silhouetted in the frame, warm fragrant air from inside the building condensing in the cold night.

Damn! His stomach clenched. Did the whole freaking building smell like her?

She looked up at him, one foot in, one foot out, stunning and anxious, as if she could read his thoughts, which, please

God, she couldn't. Her long coat was open; revealing a pale pink blouse with pearl buttons opened enough to show the round swell of ivory breasts. His hands fisted.

"Hi." She couldn't read his mind but maybe some of his sexual energy was coming through because she looked a little apprehensive. Maybe he should have taken two cold showers.

"Good evening," he rumbled in reply and she smiled, some of her tension easing.

Right response.

Good.

He could do this. He could. For a few hours at least.

She bent to carefully lock the door he had cracked in three minutes flat. She straightened and as she turned her head up towards him, perfumed strands of dark honey-blonde hair caught on the dark wool of his coat. He lifted them off carefully and they ran like silk through his hand. She watched him with wide gray eyes as if he was about to eat her up.

Nothing he'd like more. Just spread her out and dip in. Get her ready before mounting her…

He took her elbow and a deep breath. First things first. He had to feed her and strangle out some conversation before climbing on top of her.

It was going to be a long evening. The first of many long evenings.

* * * * *

"Thanks for ringing the bell and not picking the lock." Suzanne looked up—way up—at the man walking beside her down the path to the front gate.

His mouth twisted and lifted in a half smile. "You're welcome."

"I'm sure you were tempted."

"No. I'd made my point."

He certainly had.

He was so close she could see the individual drops of rain in his black close-cropped hair. What a surprise when she'd opened the door a few minutes ago. This morning he'd looked dangerous and disreputable. She'd agreed to sign a lease only because he was an officer, if probably not a gentleman.

This evening she had no problem believing he ran a successful company. Wow, did he clean up nicely. He looked just as powerful as this morning, only clad in a fine wool suit and gray cashmere overcoat, he seemed…respectable. Like someone she could be going out to dinner with, without worrying he'd eat her up and spit out the bones.

He offered her his arm as they walked down the steps, stopping under the porch covering the gate. It was raining heavily now, a steady Portland rain, out of sullen low gray clouds.

John had produced a heavy oversized umbrella but waited a moment for the rain to abate a bit before walking out into the downpour. Suzanne glanced down. He wasn't wearing combat boots like this morning, but he did have on heavy highly polished elegant shoes suitable for the rain pelting off the sidewalk.

Unlike her Rossetti pumps. She sighed. The pumps had been expensive and she was going to ruin them.

Never mind. She lifted her gaze and automatically scanned the street, as she always did.

Two blocks down and one block over was a trendy new gallery and three blocks the other way a fusion Asian restaurant was slated to open next week. Pearl was coming up in the world.

But this particular stretch of Rose Street was dark and run-down. Suzanne often hesitated before making the plunge into the street towards her car and she never went out alone after dark.

She didn't feel afraid now, though. Hand on John Huntington's powerful arm, with him by her side, she felt absolutely no fear. None at all.

"Let's go." Holding the umbrella over her with his right hand, he placed his left arm around her waist and hurried them to his car.

Truck, more like it. Suzanne looked with dismay at the open door of the passenger side of the Yukon then up at him. From this angle and in the darkness all she could see was a large jaw.

She barely had time to contemplate the distance and the impossibility of climbing into it in her tight black skirt when John swung her up in his arms and placed her gently on the seat.

She was an adult woman and he had picked her up with no more effort than if she had been a child.

Again, she had to marvel at how quickly the man could move. She was still adjusting her coat when the driver's door opened and closed quickly, letting in a swirl of cold air. He turned on the ignition.

"Where are we going?" she asked when they reached Brandon Avenue.

He cast a quicksilver glance at her. "Where you wanted." Though he didn't say the words aloud, his tone said—'*of course*.'

Suzanne blinked. "Comme Chez Soi?"

He shrugged. "That's right."

She gave a half laugh. "You were able to get reservations at Comme Chez Soi on a Friday night?" There was a permanent two-week waiting list. A last-minute Friday night reservation was impossible.

They were moving into the downtown district and she could see his clean, hard profile more clearly. His face was hard, set. "I persuaded them to make room for two more, yeah."

He'd persuaded…she caught her breath. He'd been armed. Had he pulled a gun on them?

Suzanne brought her fist to her mouth. "Oh my God, John, what did you do to them to get them to give you a table?"

He laughed, a rough low sound. "Not what you're thinking, honey. I stopped by and gave the maitre d' a note with a dead president on it."

Happy the darkness disguised her pink cheeks, Suzanne looked blindly out the window.

'Honey.' He'd called her honey. It meant absolutely nothing of course. But her heart had taken a violent leap in her chest. She folded one hand over another and took deep breaths to calm herself down.

It was like being in a cave, just the two of them. A dark cave cut off from the rest of the world. Traffic was light and the sidewalks were deserted. The big machine rode silently through the streets, leaving an arc of water in its wake. The soft whir of the windshield wipers kept time with her heartbeat.

He drove fast but well. She felt utterly safe in a secure cocoon.

"It's raining really hard," she said finally. He hadn't spoken a word in the last ten minutes. She had to learn to make conversation with this man, without her voice or her hands trembling. The weather seemed a safe topic.

"Par for the course here," he grumbled. "Rains all the time."

For a moment, she was charmed at the thought of big, bad John Huntington being disgruntled by some rain, as if he was made of spun sugar and would melt. "Well…" she teased gently. "Not all the time. There's the odd sunny day. Or two. You're not from around here, are you?"

She couldn't place the accent in his deep voice. Not western, for sure.

"No, ma'am."

He looked over and their eyes met. His gaze had such power in it Suzanne had to look away. She felt as if she had been punched in the stomach.

Say something, you idiot. "So, um, where are you from?"

He was silent a moment as he negotiated the tricky intersection off Harrison. "From all over and nowhere in particular. My dad was in the Navy and I grew up on Navy bases. Then when I was old enough to enlist, I followed in his footsteps. I've lived on most of the naval bases in this country and a good many abroad. Most of them sunny," he added wryly. "When I took early retirement, I needed a home base of my own. Weather didn't factor too much into the choice."

"So…why Portland?"

"Don't really know." He shrugged. "A lot of people told me what a great place it was. I'd met Bud years ago when he was a marine. He said there were good hunting and fishing and sailing close by. Seemed as good a place as any."

"Bud said he didn't even know you were in town."

"Yeah. I thought I was going to build my business up slowly, have time to see my pals, maybe fish and hunt some. Instead, business just took off and I've been chasing after it ever since. Haven't hardly had a chance to catch my breath. I should have looked for larger premises much earlier than this. Though - " this with a sidelong glittering glance at her that took her breath away - "I'm really glad I waited. Really glad." He swerved and parked. "Here we are."

Again, he moved quickly for such a big man. A few seconds after stopping the SUV, he was at her door. The rain had stopped and there was a hush in the air. A car whished by, headlights catching him full in the face.

She caught her breath at the intensity of his expression, deep lines bracketing an unsmiling mouth. His arms were open to lift her down. She put her hands on his shoulders and leaned forward. He did too. Their noses touched.

Something in his eyes told her he was a hair's breadth from - "Don't kiss me," she whispered.

"No." His voice was low and rough. "When I start kissing you, I won't stop. And the first time we have sex it should be on a bed, not on the front seat of a car on the open highway. So we can take our time."

He stretched out his big hands, plucked her off the seat and swung her down effortlessly.

They stood a moment, raindrops dripping from the broad oaks above them. His hands were still on her, almost spanning her waist. Suzanne's heart was pounding. She should be shocked. She was shocked. At the harsh words, at the very notion. She should say…something. Something like - "In your dreams, buster," or—"How dare you?"

The images his rough words produced—broad naked shoulders rising hot and hard above her, fevered kisses and powerful heated sex—robbed her of breath.

Power and sex came off the man in tangible waves, totally invincible, unstoppable.

She'd never felt like this in her whole life. Shaky, without bearings, like a toddler taking her first baby steps. She stared up at him mutely, their breath clouding in the chill night air, and then moved away.

"How dare you say that—even think it. Sleeping with me isn't in the lease." Her voice shook. "I don't sleep around."

His hand settled in the small of her back as he unfurled the big black umbrella over her head and started walking them towards the restaurant. "No." His voice was low. "I'm sure you don't."

Suzanne sneaked a glance up at his face. He wasn't grinning fatuously like some macho creep who'd just made a pass. His face was hard, unsmiling and serious. A soldier who'd just stated his military objective.

We're going to take that hill. We're going to have sex in a bed.

He was a multi-decorated soldier. He was probably used to gaining his objectives.

God help her, what had she let herself in for?

When they reached the restaurant, Suzanne heaved an unconscious sigh of relief, as if they had come in from more than the chilly evening. Moving into the familiar and elegant rooms, she felt on more solid ground, where she knew the rules. Where she could hold her own. In the 21st century, instead of in a cave where the man with the biggest club won.

The maitre welcomed them and showed them to a secluded corner table, one of the best, near the huge open fireplace. Suzanne's eyebrows rose. She ate often with clients at lunchtime here but they'd never been offered this choice spot. John's dead president must have been a powerful one.

"Are you familiar with French food?" she asked as she opened the large leather-covered menu.

"Yeah. Some." John shrugged. "But I'm not a picky eater. I'll have whatever you're having." He had seated himself next to her on the banquette instead of across the table and she could feel the heavy muscles of his biceps as his shoulders lifted.

Suzanne lowered the menu. "Suppose I ordered the 'Rognons à la créme ardennais?"

John settled his wide shoulders against the back of the banquette. He snorted. "You think I'd balk at eating kidneys in cream? You don't know what crappy rations we have in the field. When we're lucky enough to have rations. My men and I holed up in a cave once for three weeks and all we had to eat was a mountain goat we captured. We had to eat it raw because we couldn't afford to light a fire. We ate everything including the eyeballs. We'd have eaten the hooves and the fur if we could."

"Ugh." She shuddered delicately. "Where was this?"

His mouth quirked. "Someplace a lot more unpleasant than here, that's for sure."

"If you told me, you'd have to kill me?" she teased gently, swirling a lock of hair behind her ear.

"No. Never." He caught her hand, his face sober. "I don't hurt women, Suzanne. Couldn't. Don't ever worry about that."

He brought her hand to his mouth and brushed a kiss across the back. "But yeah. It's best for you not to know."

Her hand tingled where he'd kissed it. It surprised her, scared her.

The waiter came to slip a small plate of warm hors d'oeuvres in front of them and to take their order. John ordered in decent French. The man was full of surprises. He could pick locks, eat raw goat and speak French. An unusual combination for an unusual man.

"You speak rather well. Your French is better than my high school French, that's for sure."

"The Navy sent some of us to Monterey for intensive courses. Learning French and Spanish was okay, but Farsi and Afghani were bitches—er, tough to learn. Afghani's a good language to swear in, though. With the added benefit that no one else understands."

He didn't relinquish her hand. With the other arm along the back of the settee, he was effectively holding her in an embrace.

Suzanne cleared her throat. She had the wall to one side and the wall of his chest to the other. She couldn't see any of the other diners. He filled her entire field of vision, overwhelming her.

The flickering candle cast fascinating shadows over the hard planes of his face. He was closely shaven as if he must have shaved just before coming out. There was no hint of an after-shave but she was acutely aware of his scent just the same—clean clothes, leather and soap. And some indefinable something that must have been...him.

Suzanne coughed and fidgeted. He was so close to her she felt she couldn't pull in enough air in her lungs. She tugged gently at her hand, then harder. His large hand tightened.

"If you're trying to get me to back off, it won't work." He leaned even further forward and buried his nose in her hair. "You're too alluring for me to even think of backing off," he murmured. "You smell too good, feel too good. Christ, I want you." When his right hand moved from the back of the settee to cup the back of her neck she jumped.

"Am I spooking you?"

"A little," she whispered.

"Too bad. Because I'm not backing off. No way." He was playing with her fingers, running the rough pads of his fingers over her skin. His eyes glittered. She still couldn't figure out what color they were. Dark, but not brown. Not quite blue, either.

He relinquished her hand to stroke the back of his fingers over her cheek. "Soft," he murmured. "So soft." One large finger ran over her jawbone, then down her neck. He traced a vein that was pounding. "You might think you're spooked, Suzanne, but I don't think it's that. Do you know what I think? Hmm?"

She was breathing shallowly, her breath coming light and fast. "No." Her voice sounded husky even to her own ears. "What do you think?"

"Your skin is so fine, I can see the blood pumping through your vein here."

His finger moved tantalizingly down, stroked her collarbone, and traced the swell of her breast. He circled her nipple.

"You're hard here, honey. Like a little rock."

Through the lace of her bra, through the silk of the shirt, she felt it acutely. Felt it down to her toes. And when he brushed back and forth against her nipple she felt—shockingly—her womb clench, the fluttering prelude to an orgasm.

"You want to know what I think? I think you're…aroused."

She looked around wildly, hoping to anchor herself with something other than John Huntington, his voice and his hands. But he eclipsed everything and all she could see was his face above her, watching her as intently as any predator ever watched its prey.

His thumb stroked her nipple, his eyes watching hers. She whimpered softly and bit her lip.

"And I—" He took her hand tightly and—shockingly—placed it over his groin. "I'm aroused too," he finished in a rough whisper.

His penis felt like a steel bar, only alive and warm. She realized she had tightened her grip over him only when his eyes shuttered tight and his breath came in on a hiss. His penis jumped under her hand and became, impossibly, longer and harder.

Suzanne's hand fluttered open and she jerked it back. She folded her trembling hands on the table and stared at them. She should say something. She knew she should say something but absolutely nothing came to mind.

This was far outside the bounds of anything in her experience with men. She'd been on plenty of first dates and this was totally outside her experience -way beyond what she considered normal female-male communication.

This wasn't even supposed to be a date. They should be having a nice business dinner while discussing the details of his lease.

They should be talking about her design for his office and his plans for a new security system. They should be talking terms and utilities. Maybe with a little low key flirting under the businesslike adult conversation.

That was allowed. He was a powerfully attractive man. A very…male man. A gentle little frisson of attraction was okay. A mild flirtatious little flurry.

Not this gale force wind that threatened to blow her over.

He was sitting so close to her she could feel his body heat. A fully aroused powerful male who somehow had the capacity to make her feel as if they were alone in a cave somewhere instead of in a crowded and civilized restaurant.

Suzanne knew that somewhere out there, past his impossibly broad shoulders, was a room full of diners having a good time, eating well, and conversing in normal tones. None of it penetrated. There was just the two of them, both aroused.

He was perfectly right.

She could still feel his touch on her breast, though he'd dropped his hand. Her nipple—both nipples, actually—ached. She ached between her thighs, and knew that she'd turned wet. She'd been less aroused than this while actually making love with other men.

And the tactile memory of his penis filling her palm, hot and iron hard, swelling even larger under her touch, lingered in her hand.

It was so unlike her. Suzanne Barron didn't do sex. Not like this. Not hot and raw and so uncontrolled she'd basically fondled a man at a restaurant table.

She took a deep breath. "We need—" she licked her dry lips. Don't think about what we need. "We need to, um, talk. To talk about that new security system. And—and decorating your office, if you'd like me to take care of that."

"Okay." The heat in his eyes didn't die down and his voice was still husky with arousal. "Let's talk."

If she'd expected him to lean back and change body language, she was mistaken. A heavy forearm lay on the table in front of her. With his other arm around the back of the settee, she was still surrounded by large, warm male.

She moved, and her breast brushed his arm. A muscle in his jaw jumped.

She froze.

He drew in a deep breath. "Okay, security. The first thing you need to do is arrange for better lighting outside the building, particularly the entrance." He scowled at her. "I can't believe you live in the Pearl district and haven't taken care of any of this."

Suzanne frowned. "The entrance is lit," she protested. She'd designed the lights herself. Crystal and wrought iron in a tulip pattern.

He looked at her pityingly. "Hundred watt globes over the doorway are not what I'd call security lighting. That wattage is totally wasted, with the light going up and sideways. You don't need to light up the sky. You need light where it will do you the most good. What you've got now is pure glare that casts shadows a street punk can hide behind and ruins your night adaptation when you walk out to put out the garbage."

That kind of thinking had never even occurred to her. And never would. Not in a million years. She opened her mouth and closed it. Opened it again. "Oh."

"What you need," he continued, "is a metal halide light with no uplight and no glare. I'm going to install infrared sensor spotlights that come on only when someone walks into the viewfield of the security detectors. It's very effective for scaring intruders away."

This was an entirely new world. "Oh," she said again. "Okay."

He wasn't finished. "You'll also need motion sensors and to put your sound system on a timer so that there's music when we're out of the building."

Motion sensors. Halide lights. Detectors. "I don't know," she said uneasily. "All of that sounds expensive."

"Don't worry about it. What you designed for me will more than compensate for that."

"I didn't design it for you, specifically," she protested. "I was just doodling one day while I was sitting in the empty rooms. And I felt—*felt you were coming*." She blew out a breath. "Felt it would make a good space for a business," she finished.

"It's beautiful," he said, his deep voice quiet.

She gave him a startled glance.

"I'm only a soldier. Ex-soldier," he added wryly. "But I'm not blind and I'm not dead. What I saw was exquisite. And functional."

She smiled, flattered. "Thank you. That's precisely what good interior design is all about. When you tell me a little more about how your business works, I could probably improve on the drawings you saw."

"You'll have plenty of time to see how my business works." His eyes bored into hers. "I'll be living and working right across the hall from you."

The thought of it took her breath away. He was such a powerful presence. How on earth was she going to be able to concentrate on her work knowing he was just a hallway away?

Suzanne picked up the dessert fork and started tracing designs on the linen tablecloth. "It must have been hard to make the switch from the military to the business world. Bud told me you retired on a disability?"

She looked up briefly. Disability. It was so hard even to imagine the word disability in connection with this man. Hard, strong, tough. He looked like he could take on the world.

"Mmm." Clearly, he wasn't going to discuss anything pertaining to his injury. "It's funny. When I was in the service, I couldn't imagine any other life." He gave a half-laugh. "Shit—sorry, I'm too used to spending all my time with men, I know I have to clean up my language. Anyway, most of my life I didn't know any other life. I grew up a Navy brat and then spent my entire adulthood in the Navy. So, yeah, a lot of things are new. But you know? I'm looking forward to this new stage. I'm looking forward to building my business and to putting down roots. To having a home." His dark eyes—what was that color? The lights were too dim to tell—pinned her. "That's thanks to you. I've never lived in quarters like what you designed for me before."

Suzanne ducked her head. She'd received praise for her work before. She'd even won a prize for the design of a small museum. But nothing—nothing had meant as much to her as his quiet words.

She cleared her throat. "Well...wait until you see it done before saying that. You might not like the finished product."

"I'll like it." The deep voice was even, certain. "You about ready to go?"

Surprised, Suzanne looked around. The fire in the huge open hearth was burning low. Most of the restaurant's customers had gone. There were only a few couples left, sitting close together. Lovers. Only lovers were left. "Er…yes."

She looked down and saw that her plate was still full. All she'd done was push the food around, taking a few tiny bites. Amazing. She'd spent the entire evening at Comme Chez Soi—where the appetizers alone cost $25 and were worth every penny—and hadn't eaten.

Suzanne patted her lips with a napkin, suddenly nervous. Suddenly completely, totally aware of the fact that he was going to drive her home. Walk her up to the front door of the building, maybe inside to the front door of her apartment and…

Their eyes met and her heart lurched. "Let's get you home," he said quietly, standing up and offering her his hand.

He seemed to have some magical powers or the ability to communicate telepathically because without giving any overt signs, the waiters brought their coats and he was ushering her out with a large, warm hand at her back more quickly than she would have thought possible.

"Ah, John?" They were at the door.

"Yeah?" He smiled down at her. It was his first real smile. An amazing smile. He still looked tough, probably nothing could change that, but the smile took years off his face.

She suddenly remembered his birth date from his discharge papers. He was only eight years older than she was. He was probably much older than her—eons older—in terms of life experiences, but in terms of actual years, there wasn't that much of a gap. He was only 36. Still young for a man.

"Don't you have to pay, or something?"

The smile deepened, showing two grooves on either side of his mouth. On any other kind of face they would be considered dimples. On his face, they were…dents.

"Not necessary. I keep a corporate account here."

Oh. Well, that explained the special treatment and the magical appearance of a free table on a Friday night.

He reached around her to open the door.

It had started to sleet. Suzanne stopped and buttoned her coat up, wishing again that she'd had the good sense to wear boots. Her pretty Rossetti shoes were going to get so waterlogged.

John looked up at the sky and handed her his big black umbrella. "Here, you carry this."

"Okay." Startled, Suzanne took the heavy umbrella, wondering how she could protect the two of them when he was so much taller than she was. In one easy move, he scooped her off her feet.

"What are you doing?" she cried.

"Making sure you don't get those pretty shoes wet. Now, are you going to use that umbrella to cover us or are you going to catch the rain with it?"

With a start, Suzanne realized she'd been holding the umbrella upside down. She righted it. The only way to protect them both from the needles of sleet was to hold the umbrella behind his neck, embracing him. Her face was inches from his. Lips inches from his.

He moved smoothly down the street, carrying her easily. Their mingled breath condensed in the cold night, forming a little cloud around them.

Suzanne's cheek brushed his as they walked. This weather made for treacherous footing. It was icy out and the street was filled with puddles. If she'd had to walk the distance, she'd have made it only by moving carefully and watching her feet.

Not him. He wasn't having any problems. Even carrying her, even unable to look down at his feet, his pace was steady and sure, as if he were out on a stroll on a warm spring evening.

Suzanne's arms were around him. At first, she tried not to touch him, but the umbrella was heavy and moved in the wind. She was only able to keep it steady by bracing her right arm along his back. In a perfect position to feel the bunch and play of his strong shoulder muscles as he carried her.

His breath warmed her cheek, smelling of wine and chocolate, heady and hot. Hot. His body heat penetrated through her coat. She had to work to keep her breathing even, staring resolutely over his left shoulder at nothing at all.

They stopped and she turned her head, practically nose to nose with him. This close up, she could see features she hadn't noted before. He had a scar cutting through his left eyebrow, lifting it into an inverted V and giving him the look of a devil. His nose had been broken once, maybe twice and a very thin, white scar ran from behind his ear towards his chin, stopping just under the jaw, as if someone had gone for his jugular with a knife and had been stopped just in time.

Who knew what other scars he had on his…body.

Heat surged through her.

Oh God, think about something else, anything else. Think about the sleet and the dinner and maybe the scar over his eyebrow but not his body. Not while he was holding her in his arms, not while she could feel him, feel his body heat through who knew how many layers of clothing.

It had been bad enough wondering about his body after he'd left, when the mere thought of him naked had turned her legs to jello. It was much easier to imagine him naked now that he was holding her.

He turned his head slightly and wham. Their eyes met and she knew—she just knew—that he could tell what she was thinking. Even worse, what she was feeling. He'd felt her breast at dinner, felt her nipple.

He knew.

She stopped breathing.

They stared at each other for a second. His head dipped, and her senses went on red alert, heart thumping, but he was just reaching down for the door handle.

"There you go," he said softly, and lifted her into the passenger seat. A few seconds later, he was in the car and had started the engine.

The sleet was turning into snow, building up under the windshield wipers as he drove across town. Suzanne waited for her heartbeat to get under control as she tried not to look at him. But it was impossible.

His hard profile appeared, disappeared then reappeared as the street lights flashed by.

There was no small talk to be made. The atmosphere in the cabin was so sexually charged that there was nothing she could say that wouldn't betray her agitation. Her voice would tremble if she opened her mouth. Even her breathing was erratic.

In the end it was easier to say nothing and watch him as he easily battled the worsening weather. He was fascinating to watch. She'd be in a sweat if she had to cross town in this weather, but he was calm and relaxed, big hands easy on the wheel, movements loose but controlled.

Maybe they taught driving through sleet and snow in the Navy. Maybe he had a medal in it.

He parked just in front of the short sidewalk leading to the entrance. Snow was already building up along the wrought iron fence.

The snow muffled all sounds. When he opened her door and reached for her, it was as if the entire world had hushed so she could lean down into his arms.

Linking her arms behind his neck seemed like second nature by now.

"You don't have to carry me," she protested. "It's only a few steps."

A muscle danced in his jaw as he looked down at her. "Delighted to do it, and you're welcome."

The trip in his arms from the Yukon to the front door took forever and was over in seconds.

He put her down at the door, keeping one big arm around her, holding out his other hand. "Now's a good time to give me that copy of the key. And to give me the security code. "

"Oh, of course." Suzanne bent her head to rummage in her purse. "Seven two four six one three nine. See? I memorized it."

"Good girl." He took the key she handed him, punched in the code and opened the door.

Suzanne usually relaxed once she walked through her door, out of the dangers of Rose Street and into the warm and welcoming environment she'd created. But now she stood tensely, still half in John Huntington's arms and shivering with what she told herself was the cold.

"Turn the alarm off," he said. Her hands were shaking as she punched in the code again to finish the sequence. Only the lobby lights were on as they walked down the dark hallway. Again, he made no sound at all. The only sound was her own shoes, tapping nervously, in time with her own nervous heartbeat.

Her hallway wasn't long. Before she could gather her senses they were at her door. She rummaged in her bag and pulled out her key, holding it so hard the jagged edges cut into her palm.

Suzanne turned slightly and looked up at him.

Again their eyes met. Held.

She was acutely aware of the fact that they were completely alone in the building.

He was going to kiss her. It was there, in his body language, in the glitter of his eyes, in the tightness of the skin across his suddenly flushed cheekbones.

And she wanted him to kiss her. Her body was telling her clearly what it wanted. Her breathing was rapid and shallow. Her breasts were full and aching, her nipples painfully erect, and she tingled between her legs. He knew it. Those dark eyes saw everything, noted everything.

John's arms came up and the hairs on the nape of her neck rose. But instead of pulling her into a tight embrace, he rested his large palms on either side of her head against the brick wall and looked down at her.

Neither spoke. John bent his head slowly, eyes on hers, gaze so intent she finally had to close her eyes at the first touch of his mouth to hers.

Soft. His lips were so soft, she thought dreamily. Everything about his face seemed so hard and cold and yet his lips were so warm and soft. Gently, gently, his lips slid over hers, keeping the pressure light. He tasted so good, of chocolate and man and, intriguingly, of the wine they'd had for dinner.

Was that why her head was starting to swim? His mouth opened a little, his tongue glided over her closed lips and she opened her mouth eagerly for a better taste. His mouth lifted, then settled again, still gently. The light behind Suzanne's closed lids turned golden as her head tilted back slightly. Just enough to offer her mouth more to him.

He kissed the edges of her mouth and her lips curved slowly upwards. Who would have thought that big bad John Huntington, soldier, commando, would turn out to be such a gentle kisser? Her blood wasn't pounding in her veins anymore with anticipation and sputtering nerves. It was moving slowly through her body like warm honey.

She clutched the lapels of his overcoat, needing to hang on to something, to anchor herself. The material felt soft and warm beneath her fingertips. Just like his mouth.

His mouth moved slowly on hers, the only point in which skin touched skin. He sipped, sucked gently and her own mouth moved languidly under his. She sighed against his mouth in a haze of pleasure and opened her lips further. The soft caress of his tongue against hers electrified her, sending pleasure pulsating throughout her body.

Lazily, Suzanne opened her eyes, expecting him to look as dreamy as she felt. She jolted as she took in his expression.

Not dreamy, not tender. His face was hard, predatory, lips shiny from hers. A muscle twitched over his left cheekbone. His eyes glittered and with a small shock she finally realized what color they were. The color of gunmetal.

The fierce intensity of his gaze, so strong she felt as if hands were touching her, made her turn her head away, only to receive another shock. His big hands curled whitely against the brick wall on either side of her head. He moved his hand and brick dust drifted down to the floor.

He was clinging to the wall so hard he was gouging holes in the brick.

Suzanne brought her gaze back to his. She'd never encountered anything like this, like him, before. Every cell in her body was pulsing and alive.

That kiss had been gentle, but she had seen with her own eyes the cost to him of keeping it that way. That leashed power aroused her far more than any other man's kisses had ever done.

She could feel his body heat, coming in waves and overwhelming her. Nothing like this had ever happened to her.

She liked kissing—what woman didn't?—but it was a minor pleasure, like good food or a new dress. A kiss had never rocked her world before.

If a soft kiss, lips barely touching, a brief meeting of tongues, had her pulsing with desire, what would it be like to be held tightly as his mouth devoured hers? She'd been held tightly by him before, briefly, but long enough to feel the power of his body against hers. She'd been kissed by him, too. Gently.

She wanted to have—had to have both—at the same time. She had to know what it was like to kiss him and have him hold her tight. She wanted to feel that powerful chest against her breasts, wanted to arch against him, rub against him.

A light brief touch of her nipples in the restaurant had set off shock waves inside her. Rubbing tightly against his chest might make the ache go away. This was a degree of passion she had no idea her body could feel. She wanted more. Like a drug addict needing a fix, she stood on tiptoe, touching her mouth to his and closed her eyes.

He had aroused her in the restaurant. Everything about him excited her. His size, that air of danger, his complete…otherness from her. When his big hand touched her breast, she'd nearly jumped in her seat.

She wanted more.

She sometimes kissed a date just outside her door. Very few men made it past her door for a nightcap and even fewer into her bedroom.

Outside the door was a nice place to kiss a man goodnight. If you liked it, you could contemplate taking it a little further. If you didn't, you just whispered 'good night' and slipped into the door.

A goodnight kiss said a lot about a man and about how she reacted to that man. A nice safe testing ground.

Though nothing about John Huntington seemed safe to her.

She wanted him to kiss her hard. What would it be like to feel all that strength, all that power, all that male energy focused on her, her body tightly held close to his?

She had to find out. She wanted another kiss from him. Like before, only harder, deeper. Standing on tiptoe, she closed her eyes and touched her open mouth to his again. Her tongue came out to touch his lips and she moaned, deep in her throat.

It all happened at once. Like a whirlwind.

In a second, she was backed up against the brick wall, pinned there by his huge body. His mouth slanted over hers, hard, tongue deep in her mouth. In a second, her coat puddled on the floor and in one slashing movement, his hand moved down her front.

She heard her pearl buttons pinging on the floor and a ripping sound and then her breasts were free. She knew that because he picked her up and clamped his mouth over her nipple and suckled, hard.

The pleasure was so intense, it was almost pain and she gave a sharp cry.

He was holding her high enough so that her mound was level with his erect penis. Her back was against the wall - there was no escaping it.

He was steel-hard and ground into her, rubbing his penis over her. A hard hand reached around to her buttocks and tilted her pelvis forward until he nestled in the folds of sex and she rode him. If it hadn't been for her clothes, and his, his penis would have been inside her.

He shifted his hold and he licked his way to her other breast. His mouth was hot, avid. He licked her nipple as he suckled. Her other breast, still wet from his mouth, felt cold. She shivered.

Suzanne didn't even have time to be shocked or react in any way. Too late, she remembered his hard words outside the restaurant: 'When I start kissing you, I won't be able to stop.'

She opened her mouth to say—stop. Surely she was going to say—stop.

This was insane.

Given the type of man John Huntington was, she'd been prepared for a kiss to knock her socks off, but she hadn't been expecting this.

You've got to stop this. Had she said the words or just thought them?

And how could she ask him to stop when what he was doing was so mind-numbingly fantastic, so intensely erotic? How could she say stop when the last thing she wanted him to do was stop?

She wanted more.

He lifted his head, as if he'd heard her unspoken words and shifted her higher, until her face was almost on a level with his.

How could she ever have thought his lips soft? There was absolutely nothing soft about his face. His features could have been carved from a rock, except for his nostrils, flaring with every breath he took. They stared at each other.

This was insane. This had to stop. She gazed into his gunmetal eyes and opened her mouth to tell him. He dipped his head again, catching her mouth. His groin moved strongly against her mound, rhythmically, and she forgot everything, even her name. All she knew, all she was, was concentrated between her legs.

A flash of heat billowed up, enveloping her. Her wild cry echoed in the hallway. Just like that, she was close to orgasm, so close…she closed her eyes and tilted her head back, every sense concentrated on her loins, on the fire between her legs, just one more second and she would explode…

He pulled away.

"Not like this," John growled. "I want to be in you."

Holding her with one big hand, he reached around to unzip her skirt, pulled it down and off, then skimmed up her leg until he encountered the top of her stockings, grunting with satisfaction when he realized they were thigh-highs. His hand continued up and with one hard wrench tore her panties off.

His big hand moved between them and she gasped as she felt his touch. She was on the edge…

He freed himself and a second later drove into her.

Suzanne cried out, the sound echoing in the hallway, high and wild. His eyes bored into hers. A muscle twitched over his cheekbone. His hot breath washed over her face.

It was so incredibly, impossibly erotic. Except for her stockings, she was naked, completely open to him. He was fully dressed, except for where he was buried in her. Her naked breasts rubbed against his overcoat, still wet and cold from the outside, almost as exciting as his mouth.

His jaw muscles bunched. Still pinning her with his gaze, he pressed more deeply within her and, just like that, she exploded, shaking wildly with the force of her orgasm, shuddering and crying, pulsing wildly around him.

He moved strongly then, as if released from bonds, and started hammering into her. He was big and so rough she knew he'd be hurting her if she weren't so completely aroused.

The entire evening had been a form of foreplay, moving towards this, this wild lovemaking against a wall. Pulsing, shaking, shuddering, the explosion went on forever, until he gave a shout, grew impossibly larger and harder inside her and exploded in turn.

He clutched her so tightly she knew there'd be marks tomorrow.

Their breathing was loud in the empty hallway. His big head hung down on her shoulder. His broad chest heaved and the friction of his coat against her nipples continued to excite her body. Her treacherous body.

What had she done?

Suzanne's head slowly tilted until the back of it rested against the wall. John leaned against her so heavily she could feel the individual bricks against her back. She opened her mouth to say something—anything—but words choked in her throat.

He lifted his head. "Suzanne—" he began.

Oh God, oh God, she couldn't deal with this. Not in any way.

Whatever he was about to say—'Hey, babe, that was great, let's do it again sometime.' Or, worse, 'That was nice, but let's pretend it never happened.'—she was lost. Whatever he said, she couldn't deal with it. Her behavior had been so way off her personal radar, she had no tools, no way to cope.

"Suzanne," he said again and she couldn't tell what was in his deep voice—regret, smugness, desire—he was still hard inside her, after all—it didn't make any difference. The fact that she had no idea what he was going to say made things worse.

She didn't know what his reaction would be because she didn't know him at all. She'd only met him this morning.

He was a complete stranger.

Who she had just let make explosive love to her against a wall. Let? She'd practically begged for it.

She had to get out of here, fast.

She dropped her legs and pushed against his chest, hard.

John's head came up and he moved back a fraction of an inch. "Are you all right—" he began, and she slithered past him. She couldn't answer him, simply couldn't.

Miraculously, she still held her key in her hand. He was holding himself up against the wall with one hand, breathing hard, head turned towards her, watching her.

A twist of her wrist, and she was able to slip inside the door and close it behind her. She leaned against it, panting, eyes filled with tears.

"Hey!" His deep voice set up a vibration in her stomach and then another vibration set up—his fist against the door.

"Suzanne! Suzanne! Open up!"

Good thing she'd used top-grade lumber for those doors.

"Suzanne!" he bellowed. "Let me in!"

Suzanne tested her legs. For an instant, she thought they wouldn't bear her weight. Her legs were sore from having been opened so wide and she was sore between them from the hard rough strokes he'd used.

She stepped forward gingerly thankful her legs were holding. Passing a mirror she stopped, transfixed at the reflection. Her eyes widened.

Naked except for sheer black thigh-high stockings and heels, hair flying around her face, eyes rimmed with smudged mascara and puffy, red lips, she looked like something ordered up from Sex Kittens 'R Us.

Another thud made the door rattle in its frame.

"Suzanne! Tell me you're okay or I'm coming in! I'll give you three seconds. One..."

She shook with shock. Okay?

How could she say she was okay?

"Two!"

She'd just had wild sex. With a stranger. Up against a wall. And had had the most explosive orgasm of her life.

"Three!" Metallic sounds. He was picking the lock.

"I'm—" She could barely get any sound out through her tight throat. She coughed. "I'm okay. I'm, um, all right." She breathed deeply and raised her voice. "I'm fine. Now go away."

This was definitely a Scarlett O'Hara moment, she thought as she moved into the bathroom. She'd think about this tomorrow.

* * * * *

Damn!

John stood with his fist raised. He lowered it, and then lowered his forehead against the door.

Which put him in a position to look down at himself, wet with come, still fiercely erect and so hard he could have used his cock to knock her door down. He still wanted her, ferociously, but he'd completely blown it.

He'd been doing so well, working so hard to kiss her gently. A perfect gentleman's kiss, even though it cost him what felt like a year's supply of self control. And then she'd moaned, and moved and he'd…lost it.

Her clothes were pooled on the floor. Coat, pretty blouse with all the buttons ripped off, skirt, torn bra and ripped panties. Bending, he picked her clothes up and hung them, one by one, on the doorknob. Then he reached down to tuck himself back in his pants. He zipped up, wincing.

He'd lost the battle tonight.

But not the war.

Chapter Four

Finally, at seven the next morning Suzanne gave up any pretence of sleeping. She'd spent the night tossing and turning, angry and embarrassed at herself for how she'd behaved and even more angry and embarrassed at herself for turning red hot at the memory.

She tried to wipe John Huntington from her mind, and it almost worked, but she couldn't do anything to wipe the memory of him from her body.

All night, the ghost of his mouth on hers, the memory of his strong fingers clenched tightly around her back, his body thrusting hard into hers, kept roaring back into life, her senses feeling it as sharply as the first time.

No, sleep hadn't been an option.

She rose to the window and opened the drapes.

It was still dark outside. Though it wasn't raining now, it must have rained all night, because the snow had melted, leaving enormous puddles in the middle of the pot-holed street.

Suddenly, the street lamps that weren't broken winked off. She could see a car crossing Stuart street and could see the columns around the door of the St. Regis, a run-down turn-of-the-century building that was a flop house for the local drunks and a rent-by-the-hour place for men desperate enough to pay $15 an hour to the twin geriatric streetwalkers who ran their business out of the corner of Lucern and 15th.

If she could see the St. Regis, that meant daylight was coming.

It was already tomorrow, the day she was going to have to face the most difficult client she'd ever had, Marissa Carson, and—worse—establish some kind of relationship with her new tenant that didn't—absolutely did not—include sex.

It could be done. Sure it could.

She'd worked hard to design a home for Mrs. Carson, the Client from Hell, who changed her mind hourly. In today's scheduled meeting with Mrs. Impossible, she was going to keep her cool no matter how many fits the spoiled rich matron threw.

And she could face John Huntington The Day After like an adult, and put their relationship on a landlady/tenant basis, completely forgetting wild sex that made her hot just thinking about it.

Sure she could. Absolutely.

She passed the mirror on her way to the bathroom and winced at the view. Her hair waved wildly around her face and her eyes were ringed with dark circles. She had a red love bite on her neck. A round brush and a hairdryer would take care of the sex-and-bedhead and Erace would take care of the eyes and the hickey. But nothing was going to help the still-swollen lips and the just-out-of-bed-after-a-hot-night look. Nothing but a lot of time and space between her and John Huntington.

First a shower and some serious grooming. At some point today she was going to have to face the warrior and she needed some heavy-duty female weaponry on her side.

An hour later, she waited behind the door of her office, dressed, accessorized and perfumed, feeling like her old self. Cool, calm Suzanne Barron, staid interior decorator whose idea of excitement was matching plaid and stripes. And not Suzanne Barron, out of control sexpot.

She felt perfectly capable of dealing with John Huntington now, but she listened carefully at the door, just the same. It's not like she was trying to avoid him or anything, but eight o'clock was pretty early for anyone to start moving into a new office, wasn't it? He'd said his former office was off Pioneer Square, which wasn't close. He'd probably start moving in around ten, when she had an appointment with Todd Armstrong, her sometime partner, and before that she had an appointment with a new fabric designer to look at swatches, so she was probably off the hook for this morning. And Marissa Carson would take all afternoon, so she wouldn't be home until late.

Maybe she wouldn't see John at all until tomorrow. Tomorrow would be better. Oh, yes. Tomorrow she'd be all rested up and feeling normal and not like—like she was going to jump out of her skin.

Yes, she'd talk to John tomorrow.

Her shoulders relaxed at the thought as she put her ear to the door again to listen for noises. She listened for another minute to the complete silence on the other side of the door and with a sigh of relief pulled the door open. And froze.

The door to the rental apartment was wide open and the big room across the hallway was already stacked with what looked like a depot's worth of electronic gear. Four large men—four very large men—were marching in single file with big cardboard boxes balanced on one shoulder. John Huntington followed them, carrying a computer monitor, one of those fancy flat ones.

None of them was making a sound. Not even a whisper.

John turned at the sound of the door opening and stopped. Just stopped in his tracks and looked at her, face set. A muscle jumped in his jaw.

The effects of that pep talk to herself about how she was going to be cool, calm and collected when meeting John Huntington disappeared in a tidal wave of heat coursing through her.

God, please don't let me blush. She desperately sent up a silent prayer, but knew it was too late. She could feel the blush all the way down to her breasts, the blood pumping from her suddenly pounding heart. It rattled against her rib cage.

How could she be calm and collected when the mere sight of the man sent the blood in a hot rush through her veins?

This wasn't the first time her heart had ever pounded. Her heart rate increased nicely after a hard workout at the gym. She loved horror movies and even the 24th viewing of Night of the Living Dead could get her heart knocking.

But this was different.

The instant she'd seen John, her whole system started throbbing. Her heart set up a jungle beat. Hot and hard. Primeval, primitive. It would have been almost...exciting if it didn't scare her so much.

Her clothes, ripped and torn, hung from the doorknob and Suzanne felt her face flame even harder. Remnants of her pretty pink lace La Perla bra hung limply on top. She snatched the clothes, bundled them quickly and tossed them back into her office, shutting the door firmly behind her. But her cool resolve was gone completely.

John advanced as quietly as he always did, dark eyes inspecting her carefully. The odd color gleamed as his eyes narrowed, the color of an ancient sword reflecting sunlight.

He was just as tall, just as broad as she remembered. The effect he had on her was worse then the first time she'd seen him, because now she knew how he kissed, how rough the skin of his hands was, how it felt to have his...

No! Don't think like that or you'll implode.

"Good morning." She tried to keep her voice remote and businesslike. Landlady to tenant. Completely impersonal. She tilted her head up, aware all over again of how tall he was, how big. "You're starting early."

"Yeah. I don't like to waste time." His eyes never left hers. She was the one to look away.

The four men had deposited their burdens in the first room, gone outside, and come back in with more boxes. Still without making a sound.

"Men." John's deep voice was soft but it got results. He had his back to them, but the four men stopped in their tracks, put down their burdens, and stood stiffly to attention. "Meet our new landlady, Suzanne Barron."

"Ma'am," four bass voices said in unison.

John clamped a big hand around her upper arm, turned around and nudged her forward. Not particularly gently.

"Suzanne, let me introduce my men. You'll be seeing them around a lot. Pete, Steve, Les and Jacko." As he said their names, each man stepped forward, took her hand in his much larger one and squeezed, very carefully, for two seconds. Through all of it, John didn't release her left arm.

How foolish she'd been to think that John looked like a biker. These men looked like bikers, with torn jeans, earrings and sweatshirts with the sleeves ripped off. The last one—Jacko?—was truly frightening, larger even than John, with a shaved head—probably to make up for Les, with his waist-length French braid—sloping weight-lifter shoulders, biceps as big as footballs, pierced nostrils, and a snake tattoo from forearm to powerful shoulder. But he said "ma'am" politely, just like the others, and gently squeezed her hand with a shy smile.

"Inside, men." John said, never taking his eyes or his hand from her. "Door locked."

Just like that, they picked up their burdens and disappeared silently into John's office. The sound of the lock engaging was loud in the silent, empty hallway.

John immediately moved forward, invading her personal space. Lover-close. She stepped back, alarmed.

That was supposed to be his cue to back off, but he didn't take it. She retreated and he advanced until her back hit the wall. She closed her eyes for a second, remembering that wall. What he had done to her against that wall. How much she had loved it while he was doing it to her and how much she hoped it wouldn't happen again.

Once was quite enough.

Closing her eyes wasn't much help because she could smell him. Rain and leather and man, a smell that would forever be etched into the deepest recesses of her brain, the reptilian animal part of the brain that never, ever forgets. That smell would be associated until the end of time with the kind of wild sex no woman should ever have, for her own peace of mind. His scent enveloped her and her entire body quivered.

"Look at me. Talk to me. Are you all right?" John's voice was harsh, his hand shaking her a little, as if she'd fallen asleep. "Did I hurt you last night?"

Her eyes popped open. If she breathed deeply, her breasts would touch his chest. She laid a hand against his leather jacket. It was wet from outdoors. She pushed slightly and he stepped back just enough for her to feel a little less crowded.

"Of course I'm all right." She bit her lip. "I'm fine. Why wouldn't I be?"

"Because I was rough, and you were tight," he answered bluntly.

She blinked, his hard words evoking memories she couldn't handle. I can't do this, she thought, slithering sideways.

"No, um, no, I'm fine. Don't worry. I'm…fine. Just fine. Don't worry about it, I was…I'm…" if she said fine again she'd scream. He was looking down at her intently. How to deal with this man? She had no idea and started walking briskly towards the door, hoping to make a quick escape. He fell right into step beside her.

This wasn't going at all like the scenario she'd imagined in her head—the one where they politely said hello, how are you, wished each other good day and went their separate ways—though it very much felt like a John Huntington scenario. The one where she was kept off her guard constantly.

"I didn't use a rubber last night," he said and she stopped and closed her eyes again.

The feel of him hard and hot inside her, erupting. Afterwards, the unmistakable wetness.

Her thighs quivered. She might be trying to erase the memory of the rough, exciting sex from her mind but her body remembered. Oh, how it remembered.

"No," she said tightly, "you didn't."

"I never do that. I'm always careful. I would have told you that right away if you'd stuck around last night instead of locking yourself in your apartment to avoid me."

Suzanne bit her lip and said nothing.

"We were given constant checkups in the Navy and I never had any problems. And anyway I have a rare blood type," he continued. "I donate blood every three months and they test the blood every time. I'm clean and I haven't had sex for six months so there's no chance at all of you catching something from me."

She opened her mouth then closed it. Where was the nearest door so she could beat her head against it? She hadn't thought of disease, not once. How crazy was that, in this day and age? The man clearly messed with her head. "I'm...okay, too."

"Yes, you surely are," he said, his voice low and husky, a trace of... something in his voice. Was that a slight southern accent? "Except maybe here."

He reached out with a big hand and touched her gently on the neck, where he'd given her a love bite.

"I wish I could say I'm sorry, but I'm not. Not about any of it." He stroked her neck as she tried really, really hard not to shiver in delight, and then dropped his hand.

So much for makeup, she thought. She'd reached the front door and had her hand on the door handle. Blessed relief lay on the other side of that door and she looked at the handle longingly.

John laid a large palm against the door, holding it shut. "I want to know the second your period is late." It was said in such a commanding tone, she almost instinctively replied Aye aye, sir.

At least she had an answer for that one.

"Oh no, um, I had some...problems. I wasn't—" Suzanne drew in a deep breath and tried to gather her thoughts and the few shreds of dignity left to her. "I take the pill," she said finally. "So that's not a problem."

"The pill? Jesus." A slow smile stole across his hard face. "That's great news. Next time we have sex I can come inside you again."

There won't be a next time. The sharp words were on the tip of her tongue when she heard a car horn tooting impatiently outside. She glanced at her watch and started.

"That's my taxi. I have to go."

"Taxi?" The smile disappeared, wiped out instantly. "What taxi? Why are you taking a taxi? What's the matter with your car?"

Good question. Suzanne sighed. "I don't know. It's at the car hospital. It was making these...these wheezing sounds and stalling at traffic lights. My car's a real lemon and it's always at the garage. I took it in yesterday and they said it should be ready by tonight."

"Choking, stalling. Sounds like the carburetor went. Who's 'they'?"

"The garage. Owned by a real creep named Murphy." Just saying the guy's name made her angry. Sully Murphy was a big fat lazy slob who used his bulk to intimidate her into spending a fortune every time her car fell apart. Which was often.

The taxi driver put his hand on the horn and kept it there.

Suzanne pulled uselessly at the door handle. "I have to go now."

John was frowning down at her, his big hand still on the door. She sighed. "John, I really need to get going or I'll be late for a work appointment."

"What's the name of the garage?"

"Why on earth do you want to know—" His frown deepened and she threw up her hands. "Okay, okay, it's 'Murphy's Rental and Repair'. On 14th and Burnside."

"Give me the keys to your car. I'll make sure you get it back today and I'll make sure they did a decent repair job. This is no weather to be driving around in a car with a faulty carburetor."

He took his hand off the door and held it out, palm up. "I'll park your car out front."

Suzanne hesitated, but the truth was, she had a busy day ahead of her and it would be helpful if someone could pick the car up for her. And maybe Sully Murphy wouldn't try to snow John with arcane mechanical details in an attempt to cheat her, as he usually did with her. He sure wouldn't try to intimidate John.

Not and live.

One thing she'd learned—when it came to cars, it was still very much a man's world. If John showed up, Murphy would probably give her a big discount. Maybe treat her better from now on, thinking she had some muscle behind her.

"Okay." She dug in her purse and dropped the keys into his outstretched hand. "Tell Murphy I'll stop by tomorrow to pay. And thanks." The taxi driver was playing 'shave and a haircut' on the horn. "I really, really have to go now."

John followed her out, flipping up his jacket collar against the cold dampness. He kept a big hand on her elbow down the sidewalk right up to the taxi. He gave the taxi driver a long look as he opened the back seat door for her. But before she could climb in and slam the door shut, he stepped in front of her. She looked longingly at the cab then back up at him.

"I need to get in," she said. Low sullen clouds spat a few drops. "The meter's running and it's starting to rain."

"In a minute." He ignored the rain, which started to fall, harder and faster by the second. "I have to go out of town today and I won't be back until late. But we have to talk. Tomorrow."

Tomorrow. Great. She could handle tomorrow. She just couldn't handle today.

He pulled a pad from the inside pocket of his jacket and scribbled something down.

"This is my cell phone number, just in case you need me." He held it out to her. She took it and their hands touched. His skin was rough. She remembered his hand touching her...Trembling, she jammed the scrap of paper into her planner. "Okay."

He nodded grimly and stepped aside. "Where are you going?"

"What—now?"

"Yeah. Now."

"Downtown. Salmon Street. What are you doing?" she hissed as she slid in.

John ignored her, and laid a big arm along the top of the roof and rapped his fist sharply on the metal. The taxi driver buzzed the window down. "Yeah? You want something, bud?" he asked, bored.

John bent down and flipped the sun visor, looking hard at the taxi driver ID, and then transferring that hard look to the driver. "Listen up, Harris. The lady wants to go downtown to Salmon Street. She doesn't want to take a tour of Portland's suburbs and she wants to be there in ten minutes. Is that clear?" He had on his warrior face and it wasn't a face you talked back to.

"Yessir," the taxi driver answered, wide-mouthed. John stared at him for another long moment then slapped his hand on the roof and stepped back.

"Okay, then."

The driver took off like a bat out of hell and Suzanne didn't have the courage to look back. But she could see perfectly well in the driver's rear view mirror. John stood smack in the middle of the street, big as a mountain and looking just as immovable. He watched, scowling, in the rain as the taxi pulled away.

Men.

* * * * *

Women.

Why the hell hadn't she asked him to drive her, if her car was in the garage? Why call a taxi when she could call him? He'd gladly drive her to freaking Iceland, if she asked.

He knew why she hadn't asked. For the same reason she kept trying to slither away from him.

Jesus, he'd handled that badly. He'd meant to smooth Suzanne's ruffled feathers, reassure her that he was an okay guy, not some crazed sex maniac, because that was what she obviously thought. It was true that he'd been obsessed with the idea of taking her to bed since he'd first laid eyes on her, but he wasn't an animal.

The way she'd watched him, warily, those big blue-gray eyes wide open, ready to jump if he so much as moved, would have made him angry if he didn't know that he deserved her wariness. He was the one who'd acted like an asshole, ripping her clothes off and taking up her against a wall. Now it was up to him to make up for it.

He needed to make this right. He needed to find a way to make this right. But hell—just seeing the woman sent him into overdrive. Damn, but she'd looked pretty this morning, and even more desirable than last night, though he wouldn't have believed such a thing possible.

Still elegant, still graceful, still achingly feminine but now he didn't have to speculate about what her breasts looked like, tasted like. How soft her mouth was, how smooth her skin was, how it felt to be deeply buried inside her. He knew.

He wanted more. More of the same, only in a bed this time, with hours at his disposal to kiss that pretty mouth swollen again. He'd do it right next time, make sure she was ready, and maybe go down on her first. Make sure she was wet, and then enter her slowly. She'd been surprisingly tight.

She carried the signs of his lovemaking. Lips slightly bee-stung, a dewy sexy softness to her.

He'd given her a hickey.

He could remember every second of his mouth on her neck, the taste of her. He'd sucked hard at her skin while coming. It had felt as if the top of his head was going to explode and he was lucky he hadn't taken a bite out of her.

He'd wanted to. He still did.

He wanted to bite her, kiss her, suckle her, penetrate her. He wanted it all, every single thing she could give, and more. But if he didn't play his cards right, he was never going to get into her pants again. Right now it looked like he had better hopes of becoming a ballerina than of taking Suzanne Barron to bed. She was shying away from him as if he were the Antichrist.

He knew what the problem was but he didn't have a clue what to do about it.

It was a problem he'd had all his life, though it hadn't made much of a difference in the Navy because the Navy was full of men just like him.

But out here in the civilian world, it was a real problem. If he hadn't been so good at his job, it would have stopped him from making his business a success.

There were two kinds of people in this world. Those whose thoughts and emotions were on a dial and those whose emotions were on a switch. He was a switch man himself and had spent his entire lifetime among switches.

Something either was or wasn't. Had happened or hadn't. You either could do it or couldn't. It either worked or it didn't. You were either happy or unhappy.

Dial people were different. Their emotions ran up and down a scale and you had to guess at what point they were and try to coax them to go in the direction you wanted.

Commanding men who risked their lives in battle required a working knowledge of human psychology. John knew he was a good leader. He'd worked hard at that. But there were limits to what he could do.

His men were just as susceptible as the next man when it came to women problems, family problems, and money troubles. But soldiers had less slack to fart around. If his men had troubles John had to know—right now. He couldn't put up with bullshit and they didn't give it to him. If one of his men had a problem, John tried to help him resolve it. If it couldn't be solved, and it affected a man's performance, that man was out of the Teams. The soldier knew it, he knew it, everyone knew it.

John wasn't used to pussyfooting around or cajoling.

He'd almost lost the Western Oil contract because of his nature. The CEO, Larry Sorensen, had invited him to dinner at his house and to his golf club the next day. John knew he was being tested and he'd damned near failed the test. Sucking corporate cock wasn't his style.

Dinner had been pure unadulterated hell, with Mrs. CEO trying to plant her foot in his crotch under the dinner table and Mr. CEO trying to talk art, about which John knew exactly zero.

And the golf club episode—that had been right up there in his all-time personal list of crappy things he'd had to do in his lifetime. Worse, much worse, than an underwater incursion through the sewers of Jakarta on a hunt for a nest of tangos.

He'd had to endure Sorensen trying to bond with him while trying to smack a little white ball into a hole, just about the most useless activity the mind of man has ever invented. All of that while riding a golf cart—a golf cart for Christ's sake!—around the course.

Sorensen was at least fifty pounds overweight—all of it pure flab—and he still couldn't be bothered to walk a few miles. To top it all off, Mr. CEO talked the whole time about how his shrink had told him to 'get back in touch with his manhood'.

John wanted to tell the guy that getting back in touch with his manhood was going to take a lot more than tumbling his secretary once a month.

This wasn't his scene. He'd written off the contract until the Venezuela episode showed Sorensen and the entire Western Oil Board that actions were more powerful than words, any time.

John was good at action. Bad at words.

It had never bothered him before. Action had got him everything he'd ever wanted from life. Until now. Action wasn't going to get him back into Suzanne Barron's bed. Maybe not words, either.

But whatever it was that was going to work, he'd find it.

He'd never failed a mission yet.

Chapter Five

"Men!" Todd Armstrong said in disgust, leaning back and crossing his perfectly creased linen trousers. They were in Todd's elegant office in a steel and glass high-rise which he'd manage to make look like a boudoir. Todd's tastes were unerringly fine but classic. He could spot a Louis Quatorze at a hundred paces and he knew every auction house in the continental United States.

They made a great team. Suzanne had a natural affinity for modern design and Todd had a magic touch when it came to traditional design. Together, they buzzed. Todd kept her from being too starkly post-modern and she restrained his natural tendency to go for the Sun-King-in-Versailles-on-acid look.

"Bad date, sweetie?" Suzanne asked.

Todd's lips pursed. "I'll say. The date from hell. Listen to this one."

Suzanne sat back, prepared to be amused. Todd's forays into the wild world of dating were legendary.

"Here we are in that new Thai place—you know it?"

"The Golden Tiger?" If it was new and trendy, Todd had been there. Suzanne had just read the food review in The Oregonian and knew that it was just a matter of time before Todd would go to The Golden Tiger himself and report back to her.

"That's the one. Tacky decor but the food is to die for. At least the meal wasn't a total write-off. So anyway, here we are. Food's good. My date's cute. Hugh Grant haircut, Versace suit, tight buns. I thought it was really going to work out. And then all through the chicken satay I listen to him telling me how much he hates his mother. I'm told in excruciating detail exactly how much. Though if half of what he told me is true, he's got a point. Then he starts recounting in even more excruciating detail all about his hobby, which is?" Todd leaned back and watched her, head tilted.

She tried to think of all the things Todd might find boring. "His tax write-offs."

"Noooo. That was Tuesday's date, with the CPA." Todd shuddered delicately. "This is worse."

"Genetically modified organisms?"

Todd laughed. "No. That's actually sort of interesting. Try harder."

"Republican politics."

He held his hand up and waggled it. "Close," he said, "but no cigar. Dutch voting patterns."

"Wow." Suzanne sat back and thought about a date spent discussing a castrating mother and Dutch politics. "Pretty dire."

"The whole evening was about as much fun as rolling in glass." Todd sighed theatrically. "I'm going to give up dating for Lent."

Todd, giving up dating. Suzanne laughed at the thought. "Lent's not for another three months. And anyway, you're not Catholic. I don't think you get any brownie points for giving things up for Lent unless you are. Still, not dating for a while might not be a bad idea. Why don't you give yourself a little rest? Maybe—I don't know—maybe a week's respite?"

"Maybe," he answered, doubtfully.

Suzanne hid a smile. She knew Todd, and knew his romantic nature. He was perennially on the lookout for the man of his life. He was absolutely convinced that his soul mate was waiting for him at the next nightclub, or restaurant or cocktail party. Todd could no more stop dating than he could stop eating or breathing.

"So," she said, putting down her cup of tea after taking a sip. Delicious, perfect tea, a special blend Todd had imported especially from England. Served in the perfect teacup. Villeroy and Boch's Vieux Luxembourg. Set out on the perfect silver tray. Christofle. Placed on the perfect coffee table, made out of a 16th century monastery door. Working with Todd was a pleasure in every possible way. "Are we ready to face the Dragon Lady this afternoon? Tell you what. You bring the chair and I'll bring the whip."

"Sorry, sweetie." Todd sighed. "I think you might have to go into the Dragon Lady's lair all by yourself. My accountant says that if I don't stop by his office today, he'll report me to the IRS himself. So Marissa Carson is all yours. You can be the one to convince her that, no, that much red in the bathroom will make it look too much like an internal organ and that those 80 yards of blue shantung she ordered on special consignment from Beijing cannot be dyed yellow."

"And that you can't tear down a load-bearing wall because it bothers your—what's that dog's breed? Lapsang souchong? The one that's all hair and yaps constantly?"

"Llhasa apso."

"Right." Suzanne winced, remembering trying to argue Marissa Carson out of that one. "And as much as you'd like sun in the sun room in the afternoon, which is when you get up anyway, the sun does rise in the east, has done so for many, many years and no, there's not much you can do about that." Marissa Carson was impossible. Suzanne turned to glare at Todd. Who was going to leave her alone with a woman not even Prozac could tame. "Thanks a bunch for dumping me. Who knows what crazy new idea Marissa's hatched in the meantime?"

"She's just back from New York," Todd said contemplatively. "And crazy about the Met's new production of 'Aida'. I shudder at the thought. It probably means that now she's into—"

"Elephants," they said together and Suzanne laughed.

She sipped her tea, relaxed for the first time in 24 hours, and contemplated Todd. He was such a pleasure to look at. He wasn't much taller than she was, beautifully made, with fine features, long silky blond hair and deep green eyes. He was so good-looking that people often underestimated him.

She smiled at him and he smiled back.

Todd was such a great guy. They got along really well and had done so since the moment they'd met. They meshed so easily that Todd could finish her sentences. He knew her decorating style so well all she had to do was give a vague word picture, make the most basic of sketches and he could see her entire decorating scheme complete in his head. He had a fine sense of irony that offset her tendency to be too serious and she in turn kept him grounded.

Suzanne knew that Todd was contemplating asking her to become a full partner in his company. So far they'd only worked on the occasional contract together, like the Marissa Carson redecoration. But what they had done together had been spectacular and endlessly satisfying. Architectural Digest had taken note twice.

She was excited at the thought of joining Todd's company. He had one of the most successful decorating firms in the Pacific Northwest and it would make her career overnight, not to mention boosting her income a thousand percent. But that's not why she'd accept.

She'd accept because she couldn't imagine anything nicer than working full-time with him, with a man who understood her. Understood her feelings almost before she knew them herself. A man she always felt comfortable with, not like…

If only…

She sighed.

"You've got a lot of thoughts circling around in that pretty head of yours. Care to share?" Todd drained his tea and leaned forward elegantly to put his cup down.

Suzanne poured more tea into his cup and then hers. "Actually, I was thinking what a great couple we'd make. Just think of it. We get along really well; we like the same things and have almost the same tastes. With just enough of a difference to make it interesting. I've learned a lot about antiques from you and I've dragged you kicking and screaming into the 21st century. We never fight and…what?"

Todd was smiling and shaking his head. "Wouldn't work, sweetie. Never in a million years."

Suzanne rolled her eyes. "Well, I know that. I was just speculating—"

"No, it wouldn't work not for that reason, but for another one."

Another one? Suzanne straightened. "Well, why not? Except for the biggie, of course. I mean we really do get on, and—"

"Yes, we get along. Too well, in fact."

Suzanne smiled and shook her head. "There's such a thing as getting along too well? Wow. Have the divorce lawyers heard about that one? What does it mean—to get on too well?"

His head tilted, green eyes studying her, Todd was silent.

"What?" she asked.

"You really want to know this?"

"Of course I do. I want you to explain that thing—that getting-along-is-the-kiss-of-death thing."

"You know what I mean already, without me spelling it out for you. It's just that you won't acknowledge it. And it's the reason you haven't lost your heart to anyone and the way you're going, you never will. I know you haven't dated anyone in quite a while but when I first met you, I watched you date some eminently suitable men. Men of discernment and class, who shared your tastes in music and theater. It got to be this pattern. You'd meet a man, enjoy his company for a few evenings and then—"

Suzanne shifted uneasily on the couch. What was this? So what if her love life had been undergoing a little slump lately? She'd been busy with work, after all. Todd didn't have to make a big deal out of it. "And then?" she prompted, trying not to sound cross, trying to sound bored.

"And then, boom, you dump him. And start all over again."

Well, that was rich, coming from Mr.-Love-Them-And-Leave-Them, the man who'd taken the one night stand to an art form. She pouted. "You make me sound…shallow. And impossible to please, and—"

"Restless. And unsatisfied. The men you were dating didn't excite you, sweetie. And how could they? They were you. In male form. Talking about the Century Theater playbill and the new Scorsese film and how beige is the new black. You don't need that. You get that from me and from Claire. You're such a feminine woman, Suzanne. You need the opposite. Someone yin to go with your yang. Someone to stir your juices. Someone…someone really…male."

Suzanne closed her eyes. She knew someone who had a lot of yin to her yang. Someone who whipped her juices into a froth. Someone really, really male.

"Someone tall, and dark and with shoulders out to here," Todd's baritone continued dreamily. "With short black hair just faintly silver at the temples, that early Gianni Agnelli look, you know? And eyes to die for. Yum."

Suzanne's eyes popped open at that and she glared at Todd, sitting smugly on his Sanderson cabbage rose couch. She would have thrown a pillow at him, but she might miss and tea stains were hard to get out of silk.

Todd smiled knowingly. "Food's really good at Comme Chez Soi, isn't it? It's that new chef of theirs. But then how would you know? You didn't eat a bite."

Chapter Six

The taxi left her at her gate. Suzanne paid him then looked across the street. Her car was parked right there. On an impulse, she walked over and got in, resting her hands for a moment on the steering wheel. At the first turn of the ignition key, the car started right up without that choking, grinding roar she'd grown used to. It purred gently, powerfully. She sat there, pleased, listening to her car hum, healthy and whole.

Her car was back from the dead and better than ever, thanks to her tenant. Her sinfully sexy tenant.

She'd overreacted. Yes, they'd had sex and that was at least as much her fault as his. It's not like he'd overpowered her or anything. The instant his lips had touched hers, she'd melted. And though it had been rough it had also been exciting. Certainly more exciting than anything she'd experienced in…ever.

Suzanne had no doubt whatsoever that if, instead of bolting in panic back into her apartment, she'd asked John in, he would have followed right on her heels and they would have spent the rest of the night…what?

Making love, no doubt about it. In a bed. Instead of having sex. Against a wall. And in between bouts, they'd have talked. Maybe laughed a little, opened that bottle of Chablis she'd had in the fridge for weeks, finished the jar of contraband caviar a client had brought her.

John had flubbed it but so had she. She'd run from him like a scared rabbit.

And it wasn't as if he'd blown her off the next day. He'd immediately acknowledged her, taken responsibility, said they needed to talk.

And the biggie—he'd dealt with Murphy for her and picked up her car. Which now purred beneath her hands. Pleased, she switched off the ignition and sat there, feeling a little foolish at her reaction to him.

A sudden vision of John Huntington formed before her eyes. His size, his strength, his intensity, his brute male power. Nope, she hadn't overreacted. The man was formidable in every way.

She thought about what Todd had said as she opened her gate and walked to the door. That maybe the men she'd been dating had been too predictable, too bland, too...safe.

What was wrong with safe? She thought as she disconnected the alarm, opened the door, and then switched the alarm back on, just as John had made her promise to do. Safe was nice, warm, comfortable. Not words she'd ever associate with John Huntington.

He threw her for a loop.

He'd occupied most of her headspace all day. All day yesterday, too. Every second, in fact, since she'd met him, and that wasn't good. She was a busy professional, just about to make that leap into the spheres of the very successful and she didn't have time for obsessions. She barely had time to date, so what little time she had should be with men who would stay nicely in the background where they belonged and wouldn't occupy her every waking moment.

Like now, walking warily into her own building. Wondering if he was in. Hoping he wasn't. Hoping he was.

He wasn't here. She paused for a moment in the hallway. He was a quiet man, almost eerily so, but she knew her building. It held the stillness of emptiness. And come to think of it, she hadn't seen his Yukon parked outside.

From the sudden certainty of that, Suzanne realized that she'd been subconsciously looking out for his SUV and listening for signs of him. He'd said he'd be out of town this afternoon and would be late getting back. So she'd see him tomorrow.

Which meant that she definitely needed a good night's sleep if she wanted to face him with anything approaching equanimity.

To get that good night's sleep she had to put Commander John Huntington right out of her head. She had to get her life back.

Tomorrow. She'd get her life back tomorrow. Today had been much too exhausting. Marissa Carson had topped herself today, changing her mind about everything that had been decided upon up until now. Most of the furnishings had already been ordered. When Suzanne pointed out that she'd lose a lot of money, Marissa had tilted her lovely head back and laughed long and hysterically, saying she was soon going to be very rich.

Marissa had been feverish, jumping out of her skin. Suzanne imagined that she was having problems with Mr. Carson, whom she'd never met. But she knew what he looked like. Pictures of him, a handsome, blond, cold-eyed man, were pasted all over the apartment. Had been pasted. Now all the photographs of him had been either taken off the walls or placed face down on the coffee table. Clearly, there was trouble in paradise. That was confirmed by the tall, blond, cold-eyed man who'd nearly knocked her over as she was exiting Marissa's building a few hours ago. He'd looked furious and Suzanne was sure that fireworks were in the offing.

It had been difficult to absorb Marissa's hysteria while trying to deal with her wishes for her apartment, which changed hourly. They'd finally agreed to meet again in two weeks, when presumably Marissa would have a better grasp on what she wanted.

In the meantime, Suzanne had spent an emotionally exhausting afternoon and had had to skip lunch, which made her cranky.

Her evening ritual calmed her, soothed her. A hot bubble bath with lavender oil. A bowl of frozen minestrone heated up in the microwave, a glass of red wine, half an hour in bed with the latest Nora Roberts and lights out at ten.

Suzanne closed her eyes, savoring the clean linen sheets, the warm light eiderdown, and the stillness of the night. The weather forecast had been for snow and she'd opened the curtains in all the rooms because she liked snow. As she snuggled deep in her bed, sure enough, a few stray snowflakes were drifting down from the sky, visible in the halo of the streetlights. She could feel her muscles start to relax, feel that slow slide into sleep…

Which didn't come.

Two hours later, the grandfather clock in her living room next door tolled midnight. She listened to the slow tock and whir of the mechanism, and then the solemn chimes. She counted twelve and sighed as she slipped her legs out of bed.

The night was beautiful. Low-lying fluffy white clouds, like a child's vision of Christmas, hugged the tops of buildings. Fat, lazy cartoon flakes floated down, gently, as if they had all the time in the world.

Snow was kind to her street. It covered the ruts and cracks and potholes. It softened the buildings grown raggedy with age and neglect. It spread its gentle mantle over this part of town, abandoned and sometimes violent, full of unhappy, failed souls.

The night sky glowed, reflecting the bright lights of downtown off the low-lying clouds. The clouds shimmered and snowflakes danced. Suzanne watched for a few minutes, searching elusively for peace.

Like sleep, it wasn't coming.

She felt edgy and unsettled, as if she had somehow crossed a divide without meaning to. Without even wanting to. Moved into a new part of her life where she didn't know the rules.

Todd's words kept coming back to her. It was true—she had always dated men with whom she knew she could keep the upper hand and it was also true that there was no question of her keeping the upper hand with John. He was a dominant male in every sense of the word.

Of course, they weren't exactly dating. One evening out, one bout of sex... what was the word for that? Dating? She had no idea; it didn't fit any of her neat categories. And to top it all off, they were living together. Or rather not living together, but living in the same building. Just the two of them.

John was like a tiger. A gorgeous, wild animal that needed to be approached gingerly because it could rip your heart out without even trying. You needed to keep your distance from beautiful, wild animals. How was she going to do that when she would be seeing him every day?

The silent night wasn't offering up any answers, just gentle snowflakes slowly tumbling out of the shimmering clouds. A light played erratically against the low hedge of box trees, which ran along the side of the building, and Suzanne watched it flicker and glow against the dark leaves.

She peered more closely.

Why was it doing that? Where on earth was the light coming from? Not downtown, that was for sure. Not against her hedge.

And the light wasn't a shimmer but a pinpoint glare. She frowned. A car? No, the beam was too small and it jumped around. And anyway it was coming from inside the hedge not from the street outside. At that angle, it had to come from...her house! From her office.

A fire!

Suzanne's heart leaped in her throat as she ran to the door, ran through the living room and kitchen without bothering to switch on the lights. Each room had big picture windows and she watched the shiver and play of the light against the hedge as she went from room to room.

The little circle of light kept flickering on and off and she stopped, hand on the door that would take her into her office. Her mind was just catching up with her body.

What was she thinking? Was she crazy?

No fire would make that kind of light. A fire's light would be steadier, and bigger. There was only one thing that would make a light like that. A flashlight.

And a flashlight meant…someone was in her office.

Thank God she was barefoot. She hadn't made any noise. Whoever it was in her office can't have heard her.

The door to the office was ajar and she carefully pulled her fair hair back from her face and peeped around the corner.

There was nothing to see at first, just the blackness of a large dark room. Then there was a bumping sound, like a human limb meeting a piece of furniture, and a soft curse. If she hadn't actually had her head practically in the room, she wouldn't have heard it.

Someone had broken into her house.

A man. The low pitch of the curse had been unmistakable. Then a dark form crossed the window, perfectly silhouetted against the brighter night sky and Suzanne's heart stopped. Then started again, pumping hard. She had to clench her teeth to keep from gasping.

The intruder was tall, lanky, with longish hair brushing his shoulders, holding a pencil flashlight in one hand. The flashlight was the source of the light she'd seen spilling out the window.

In his other hand, he was holding a big black gun.

Oh God, oh God! She thought, taking an involuntary step backwards. Another curse, low and vicious came from the room. He had tripped over another piece of furniture.

Her office was complicated, almost over-decorated, which she'd done deliberately as an advertising tool, showcasing what she could do. It was almost impossible to navigate if you couldn't see. The man was finding the furniture pretty much by touch. Or by banging his shins.

He had a gun. A burglar with a gun. Hadn't she read somewhere that burglars don't carry guns? That they know that the penalty for breaking and entering is much less than that for armed robbery. That they have a different psychological profile from other criminals and are basically non-violent.

All a burglar wants, the article said, is to get in, get as much of your expensive stuff as possible, and get safely back out.

Except he wasn't doing that. The flashlight picked out her brand-new Bang and Olufsen, worth a lot of money—worth more, actually, than she could afford—then moved steadily on. It skimmed over her collection of antique silver frames collected by three generations of Barrons, which an appraiser date once said, was worth more than her new car. It lighted briefly on the original Winston Homer great-Granny Bodine had bought from the great man himself. Suzanne had used it as collateral for the mortgage.

The flashlight didn't even linger over these items, but just kept roaming over the walls. Looking for something.

Looking for what? It was a poor part of town. There weren't many buildings containing what the burglar had just skipped over as unworthy of stealing. What else could he possibly be looking for?

And just like that, Suzanne knew.

The burglar wasn't there to steal her hi fi or her frames or her paintings.

He was there for her.

He was armed and on the hunt. Hunting her. For some unknown reason this man with the gun wanted to kill her. That was why he'd broken into her house and why he was ignoring all the valuable objects he could steal without any trouble at all. He didn't want them. He wanted her and he was going to get her because there was no way out of the building except past him.

Her home was four big rooms, one after the other, and only the last one, her office, had a door leading out into the corridor. The rest were internal doors, and all the intruder had to do was go through them, one after another, until he found her.

The windows were alarmed and bulletproof. Opening a window would set off the alarm system, which could only be disengaged at the front door. There was no hope of breaking a window and crawling through. The man who'd sold her the windows had given her a demonstration of what bulletproof meant. He'd taken her to the company's underground test room and fired a gun at a test windowpane, which had starred but hadn't broken.

No way could she get through.

The closest police station was downtown. It would take them at least a quarter of an hour to get here and by then, the intruder would have gone through all the rooms, would have found her and…

John!! Only John was close enough—and tough enough and dangerous enough—to help her. If he was home.

Please be back, John, she prayed, running swiftly, silently, back through the kitchen, the living room and into the bedroom. She quietly closed each door, locked it, and then ran to the next.

The locked doors wouldn't hold back a man capable of getting through her security for long, but maybe it would buy her a few minutes if he was trying to be quiet and not attract attention. All she needed was enough time to call John for help. If he was here, he was only across the hallway.

And if he wasn't?

I'll be home late, he'd said. What was late? Had he come back in while she'd been trying to sleep? Was he sleeping just a few feet away? Or was he still out of town, completely unable to answer her call in time?

Please don't let him still be out of town!

She was sobbing as she locked the last door, the door to her bedroom. She was now as trapped as a mouse in a cage. If the intruder reached her bedroom, there was nowhere else to go, nowhere else to hide.

Fumbling, crying, she reached for her purse and with fingers that felt as thick as sausages rummaged for her cell phone. Her hands were shaking, useless. With a curse, she upended her purse, rummaged madly then—with a sob of relief—found her cell phone. She grabbed it and switched it on.

Her throat was raw from the panicked breaths she was gulping in. She held the phone in one hand as she frantically went through the seeming thousands of bits and pieces of paper in her purse with the other.

Damn! She was usually tidy, but she'd been so busy lately she hadn't had time to clean her purse out. It looked like every number she'd ever known was written down on a small piece of paper. There it was! No, that was the number of her tax advisor. Old high school friend she'd bumped into at Nordstrom's, antique dealer, and new hairdresser—all of them had scribbled their numbers on scraps of paper.

Think, Suzanne! She commanded herself. She closed her eyes, jaw clenched, and tried to think past her pounding heart and shaking nerves back to when John had written his cell phone number down.

If the intruder had found her kitchen door and picked the lock, he'd already walked through it. It was basically an open space. No obstacles at all. He could already be in her living room, or worse. Maybe he was already at the bedroom door.

She whimpered. *Think!!*

Cold, it had been cold outside. John had stood towering over her, angry with her because she'd called a taxi, writing his number down—she remembered his handwriting—bold, black, and distinctive—and she'd stuck it in…

Her planner!

Frantic, she scrambled for it, flipped through the pages and…there it was!

Shaking, she punched out the number, hoping she was getting it right on those awkward buttons. Hoping her shaking hands wouldn't betray her. The phone buttons seemed so hopelessly small. What if she'd punched the number in wrong?

Ah. The line connected and started ringing. Make it be the right number, she prayed.

One…

Did she hear a small thud in the next room? Oh, God.

Two…

Come on, come on!

Three…

"What's the matter, Suzanne?"

She nearly dropped the phone in relief at hearing that deep voice. So calm, so matter of fact. Some part of her was glad that he seemed to be always a step ahead of her. He had caller ID and already knew that she wouldn't be calling him after midnight unless she had a problem.

"John," she whispered. "Where are you?"

"About three blocks away," he replied. The deep tones seemed to vibrate through the phone. Just hearing his voice made her feel better. Less panicky. "Why?"

"Please hurry. There's a man in the house. He was in my office a few minutes ago. John, I don't think he's a burglar. He wasn't trying to steal anything and he's—he's armed."

"Where are you now?" His voice was still calm, but she could hear a deep rumble in the background as he gunned the engine of his SUV and the squeal of tires as he rounded a corner.

"In the bedroom," she whispered. She clutched the phone with wet hands, as if it were a lifeline. "The last room down. I locked the door."

"Okay, this is what I want you to do. Put a chair under the handle. Don't move furniture—that would make too much noise. Unscrew the lightbulbs on the lamps. Do you have a walk-in closet?"

"Y-yes." She got the word out through chattering teeth.

"Get in and lock the door to that from the inside. Move to the very end and wait there for me. I'm coming. Do you hear me, Suzanne?"

"Yes." Her voice shook. She bit her lips. "Hurry," she whispered and broke the connection.

She only had one chair and placed it under the handle. It was pretty but flimsy. By the time the intruder made it to her bedroom door, he might not be worrying any more about making noise. The chair would hold a determined man back only a few seconds. She quickly unscrewed the light bulbs from the three lamps in the bedroom before heading for the closet door.

For the first time in her life, Suzanne cursed her tidiness as she locked the door behind her. How much better it would be to crouch in a tangle of old jeans, ratty tee shirts and discarded dressing gowns, instead of the bare floor of her superneat closet trying to hide behind two rows of shoes, neatly lined up and no defense whatsoever, unless you counted the killer stilettos on one pair of Manolo Blahniks which she'd bought in a moment of insanity and had never worn.

She crouched and waited. And bitterly regretted that she'd never taken a self-defense class, though she wasn't sure what she could do against an armed man.

Wonder Woman would have known what to do. So would Xena the Warrior Princess. And Charlie's Angels. They'd have known how to disarm an armed man and then they'd kick butt, but there were three of them and only one of her.

She moved slightly, brushing a lavender sachet dangling from a satin ribbon she'd hung from the rod. She closed her eyes in the dark, breathing in the sharp scent. She'd made the sachet herself from lavender gathered in her parents' retirement home in Baja. It smelled of summer gardens and sun and earth. Her hand touched a cashmere shawl she'd worn to a production of *The Mikado* with Todd. She fingered it, taking comfort from the softness and warmth.

She didn't want to die.

She wanted more summers with her parents, more theater evenings with Todd. More summer picnics, more skiing vacations. More evenings out, more evenings in.

More.

Life was so sweet, so rich, the highs and lows of it. She loved her parents, she loved her home, and she loved her friends. Her career was just taking off. She was going to live a hallway away from the sexiest man she'd ever seen. She'd been shocked at the sex they'd had, but it had made her feel alive in every cell of her body. She wanted more.

She didn't want to die. Oh, God, she didn't want to die.

How far away had John been? Three blocks? Even driving fast, how quickly could he get here? Was he parking now? Running towards the house?

With a sudden disconcerting sense of certainty, Suzanne knew that as fast as a human being could make it—that's how quickly John would come for her. Whatever could be done to protect her against an armed intruder—that's what John would do.

There was no one else in the world right now she'd rather have coming to her rescue than John Huntington.

Where was the intruder now? Her living room was very decorated, too, with two sofas, armchairs, occasional tables, footrests, floor vases scattered all over. If the intruder wanted to proceed stealthily, all the objects in the room would slow him down considerably.

If he didn't care about making noise anymore though, then he was moving fast. Had he simply turned on the lights, tired of bumbling around in the dark? If he knew she was home, then he also knew there was only one other place she could be. If he wanted to, he could break down her bedroom door, wrench open the closet and shoot her in the space of a minute.

What was that noise? Every muscle tensed and her breath left her body in a rush. Her mouth was bone dry.

It was so horrible huddling here in the dark like a fox hounded to earth. Her heart was pounding so hard it seemed impossible that it wasn't making a noise. It sounded loud to her. Surely it could be heard in the next room?

She wiped her face on her sleeve. Whatever happened, she needed to be able to see. Even if it was only the gun that would end her life. She swiped at her eyes as she bit down on her lips and ordered herself to stop crying. To stop trembling. She pressed her hands between her knees so she could tell herself her hands weren't shaking.

She never knew she was such a coward. How could she have known? She'd never faced danger—real danger, as opposed to the danger any woman living alone is subject to every day—in her life.

I don't want to die, she thought again as she rested her forehead on her knees. A tear dropped on her knee and ran down her calf.

She waited in the dark, endlessly.

Her watch was on the bedside table. She had no idea how much time had passed since she'd spotted the intruder. Since she'd called John. Ten minutes? Two minutes? Half an hour? There were no bearings here, in the muffled scented darkness of the closet, no way of telling time except by her thudding heart.

Had she sent John to his death? He hadn't even hesitated, had simply said he was on his way, but should she have called the police instead of him? She might well die, but she might go down having brought another man to his death. A good man. A man who willingly stepped into danger for her.

Right now, he might be out there, bleeding, dying…

Somehow, that was the worst thing of all.

Suzanne straightened abruptly. That had definitely been a sound. Like something heavy falling. A piece of furniture? A…body? The sound came from the living room, right outside the bedroom door. A long moment of silence, while she strained her ears.

And then another sound, metallic this time.

Someone picking the lock.

Suzanne wiped her eyes. Whatever was going to happen in the next few seconds, she wanted to be clear-eyed.

A scraping…the chair was pushed out of the way. Suddenly, light flooded through the louvered slats of the closet door. A shadow fell across the door.

Suzanne waited, dry-eyed now, breathing slowly. Trying crazily to brace herself against a bullet. She scooted as far as she could go against the wall, pressing against the wooden slats with her shoulders, wishing she could push herself through to the other side.

The closet door opened and a man filled the doorway. Broad shoulders barely cleared the frame. A killer's face—lean cheeks, cold gunmetal eyes, hard mouth. He looked at her with narrowed eyes, a large black gun in his hand.

With a glad cry Suzanne rushed into his arms.

Chapter Seven

John's arms closed around her fiercely.

Suzanne was trembling, trying hard not to cry. Shaking, breathing raggedly. Soft and warm and—thank you, God—alive.

John covered the back of her head with his right hand and wrapped his other arm around her waist, holding her tight, trying to give her the animal comfort of his body. Pressing her close to still those awful tremors.

She was frightened to death. So was he. He couldn't remember being this scared, ever. Not in the fiercest firefight.

He hadn't been frightened for himself. The takedown had been smooth, a textbook SEAL operation. The bad guy hadn't even known John was there until he was uselessly tugging at the knife cutting through his throat. But until this moment, until he had his arms tight around Suzanne's slender body, John hadn't been sure he'd got here in time. Hadn't been sure he wouldn't find Suzanne lying in a pool of her own blood…

He'd been driving home, content with the day's work advising a bank in Eugene on security, with a five-year consultancy contract in his pocket. If business continued like this, he'd have to expand again. For the third time in six months. Maybe call in a few other guys from his team who were up for retirement.

He'd had to retire early because of the damned knee injury, but he probably hadn't had more than another seven, eight years of active duty left in him anyway. In his line of work, you either died on the job or retired early. It's wasn't a job you aged in.

The Teams took everything a man had—and then sucked up some more.

If he expanded again, he knew exactly who to call. Senior Chief Kowalski was up for retirement and would make a perfect employee, maybe some day a partner. Super-smart, skilled, honest—and looking like something out of a horror movie. John smiled at the thought of introducing Suzanne to Kowalski, though she hadn't turned a hair on her lovely head at meeting Jacko.

Despite her fragile appearance, Ms. Suzanne Barron seemed pretty sturdy. And smart and beautiful and with it. Oh yeah, she'd do just fine. All in all, John had been well pleased with himself while driving home.

Home.

When was the last time he'd ever felt a place was home? As opposed to a bed to bunk in? Yet 437 Rose Street had instantly become home. And that was before the delectable Ms. Barron decorated his working and living quarters.

He couldn't wait for that, odd in a man who never cared what anything in his surroundings looked like. His major color scheme all his life had been olive drab. But now he found himself really looking forward to living in what he'd seen in those drawings. Those rich muted colors, those sleek elegant lines—hell yes, he could get used really fast to working out of an office like that. It would be a pleasure. He couldn't wait for her to start.

Yes, he'd been definitely revved as he drove back through the rain. He was living in the same building as the most beautiful and desirable woman he'd ever seen. They'd already had explosive sex and getting back into her bed—back into her, it didn't have to be in a bed—was just a matter of time. And to top it all off, he was well on his way to becoming rich and successful. Life just didn't get any better than that.

And then Suzanne had called and he'd instantly gone to Defcon 1—the highest state of alert.

He'd known the instant he'd seen the number on the screen that something was badly wrong. Suzanne wouldn't call him at midnight unless she was in trouble—and she was.

A man in her apartment. An armed man. It didn't take SEAL training to know what that meant. Burglars don't carry weapons. Burglars are nice gentlemanly criminals. All they want is to infiltrate your house, politely relieve you of your expensive worldly possessions and get quietly back out. No guns. No violence. The alternative was a hophead, crashing into Suzanne's house hoping to boost her hi fi or TV for resale to the local fences to make enough for the next fix. But druggies weren't organized. A hophead wouldn't be slinking, trying not to make noise.

No, the scumbag in Suzanne's house was there for one purpose only. To take her out. Any intruder who was bypassing the silver, artwork and fancy electronics in her study was out for much bigger game—blood. Suzanne's blood.

Not while John could draw a breath.

His hands had clenched hard around the steering wheel as he braked to a stop a block from the house, around the corner and out of sight. The son of a bitch was armed. Well, so was he. Sig Sauer and knife and determination. Those three weapons had prevailed against some of the most dangerous men on the planet.

In the office, Suzanne had said. Only that had been minutes ago.

The level of alarm ratcheted up a notch at the front door. The intruder hadn't just broken through the security system—he'd wrecked it. And taken out the telephone system, too, while he was at it. Thank God Suzanne had had the presence of mind to use her cell phone instead of the landline to contact him.

The guy hadn't exactly been an amateur. Disabling an Interloc system and the phone lines took a little bit of knowledge. But he hadn't been expecting much resistance. John had heard him almost immediately, in what Suzanne used as a living room. He could hear him two rooms down, crashing around like a bear in the woods.

Using the Sig was out. John didn't know if the guy had body armor, which meant the usual double tap to the head wasn't an option—his weapon would wipe the guy's face off entirely and John wanted an ID. He wanted to see the face of the son of a bitch who was threatening his woman.

That left the K-Bar.

John had excellent night vision. He moved swiftly and silently through the room into the next one. A kitchen. Empty. Oh Jesus, Jesus. Suzanne's living quarters were a replica of his. Four rooms. Her bedroom was the last room down, she'd said. One more room to go.

Except the son of a bitch might not be here. He might have already wasted Suzanne and left. John moved more quickly, silently entering the next room and…there he was! Gun up, at the bedroom door, hand out for the doorknob.

He still didn't have a clue anyone else was in the house. He died not having a clue, face down to the floor, John's K-Bar through his throat.

John turned on the lights, crossing the room quickly as the man flopped for two, three seconds, feet drumming, on the floor. Blood spurted, sprayed. John watched, cold-eyed, as the man bled out fast all over the hardwood floor, then stilled in the unmistakable sprawl of death. John looked down at him for a long moment, thinking.

Next to the couch was the Portland phone book. There were two pages of Morrisons but only one Tyler Morrison. He dialed the number with his cell phone.

"Morrison." Though it was very late, Bud sounded alert. John knew he would sound that way even if he'd been roused from a deep sleep.

"Bud, John here. Huntington." John kept his voice low.

Bud didn't waste time on small talk. "What's up, John? You in trouble?"

"Might say that. I just killed a man." John heard sheets rustle and a soft woman's voice murmuring in the background. He remembered Suzanne saying Bud was dating a friend of hers. "Sorry to wake you up at this hour, Bud, but I need to call this in. I'm in Suzanne Barron's building on Rose Street. She had an intruder tonight. Armed. I took him down. You'd better get over here with your team. It's not pretty."

Bud put his hand over the receiver and John could hear muffled soothing noises. He came back on line. "I'll be right over." Bedsprings squeaked. "I'll call it in and go directly to Suzanne's house. The rest of the squad will be there in about a quarter of an hour."

"Door's open," John said. "Wide open. He trashed the security system. And you can use the sirens. He's not going anywhere. Hang on a second, Bud."

John hunkered down to study the dead man.

The crime scene squad would be here soon and John knew better than to disturb the scene, but what he was able to see was bad news. The intruder had dropped his flashlight and gun to claw at his throat. The gun was a silenced .22 Colt Woodsman. A raw-looking rectangle on the side told its own story. John's jaw clenched.

A Colt Woodsman was the standard assassin's gun.

John's fists closed at the thought of a .22 bullet hitting Suzanne. The .22s were subsonic rounds, perfect for silencers. You can get in close with a .22. The bullet is guaranteed to bounce around inside the victim's body doing massive damage instead of passing through. He pushed out of his mind what a headshot would have done to Suzanne and spoke into the phone.

"I think we've got ourselves a hired hand here, Bud."

"Yeah? How so?"

"He's got a Colt Woodsman with the serial number filed off. With a suppressor. You don't carry a weapon like that to make off with the silver tea service." John rapped a knuckle on the guy's shoulder. It echoed hollowly. He'd been right. "And he's got body armor. That's not standard B & E fare, either." Something prickled on the back of John's neck. He knew that prickle, trusted it, and it wasn't good. "Hurry it up, Bud."

"On my way, big guy."

John hung up, picked the bedroom lock, easily dispensed with the chair under the handle and screwed in the light bulb on the lamp nearest the door.

Good girl, he thought as he saw the closet door on the other side of the room. She'd followed his instructions to the letter.

He picked the lock on the closet door and looked inside. Two huge gray eyes in a white face looked up and he felt something in his chest clench hard. They stared at each other for a long moment then Suzanne launched herself into his arms. He held her close, closer.

She was safe.

And she was going to stay that way.

* * * * *

Suzanne couldn't stop trembling. Finally John held her so tightly against him it was as if he absorbed her shock into his system. She was able to draw in a deep breath for the first time in what felt like hours.

"Better now?" His voice was a deep rumble against her ear. She nodded jerkily.

"Yeah," she whispered. Biting her lips, she stepped back.

"Good," he grunted. He held her at arm's length and looked her over carefully. There was absolutely nothing lover like in his gaze. It was cool, impersonal and very thorough. Suzanne understood he was studying her to judge what shape she was in.

Well, she was alive, for starters, thanks to him. That was good, that was certainly better than she thought she'd be a just few minutes ago. The panic was subsiding and any second now she'd get her trembling under control. She tried on a smile and he nodded and dropped his arms.

It hadn't been much of a smile but it seemed to satisfy him because he was backing away, while taking in her room, observing everything carefully, then moving on. Looking for another intruder, maybe? He still had a gun in his hand. He held it loosely, barrel pointed towards the floor, but he held it like an extension of his hand. He stood lightly, almost on the balls of his feet like a dancer limbering up. She got the impression that he was ready for anything. That nothing would or could catch him unawares.

He pushed open the bathroom door, gun up beside his ear, a lightning-quick perusal inside, and then closed it. Moving quietly, he checked everything, every point danger could come from, before coming back to her. He was studying her again, taking in her nightgown and bare feet.

"I called it in, so the police will be here soon. You might want to put some clothes on. Dress warmly and comfortably. Pants, sweater, boots. And Suzanne, while you're at it, put together a small case with a couple of changes of clothes."

Small case? Changes of—Why? She started to ask but then looked at the grim expression on his face.

O-kay.

He'd come to her rescue, big time. She could pack a bag.

"All right," she said quietly and he nodded. Pleased at her acquiescence, but with that air of…remoteness about him, as if he were listening to sounds in the distance.

And now she heard it too. A siren, faint at first, then two, quickly rising in tone, almost unbearably loud until they were suddenly cut off. Two police cars, lights flashing, stopped in front of her building and the muffled slam of the car doors filtered through the night air. Another car pulled up behind them and a tall, familiar figure climbed out.

The cavalry had arrived.

"I'll wait outside," John said as he disappeared through the door. "Hurry."

Suzanne quickly dressed. She did exactly what he'd said, and pulled on a thick heavy sweater, comfortable wool pants and cold-weather boots. Pulling her small suitcase on wheels out of the closet, she packed quickly. Again, exactly what he'd said. Two pairs of pants, three sweaters, another pair of boots, underwear and two nightgowns. Beauty case on top and she was ready.

There were low voices in the other room, but everyone stopped talking as she opened the door. Suzanne stepped into the living room, pulling her suitcase behind her, then stopped.

Just stopped, and stared.

He had fallen to the right of the door. Any further to the left, and he'd have blocked it.

The only dead body Suzanne had ever seen was Granny Bodine, who had died peacefully in her sleep at 93, gently laid out in her casket. This man hadn't died peacefully.

He was sprawled facedown on the floor, hands curved into claws, one clutching the big black blade handle sticking out from his throat. The knife must have severed the jugular. Blood pooled under the head of the man and sprays of it surrounded the body.

Suzanne took a deep breath, then another, desperately trying to get her stomach under control. She blinked, as the dead man seemed to rise up from the ground and float towards her. A dull roar filled her ears.

A hard hand cupped her neck, pushing her head gently down. "Breathe."

She didn't need to see him to recognize John's voice, recognize his touch. Obediently, she bent and tried to breath past the shakiness. Slowly the stars before her eyes receded.

There were people in the room, talking, moving around, but she only registered John's presence. Large and solid beside her. "Come on now, breath deeply."

She swallowed heavily and looked away, down. Breathed. Deeply. In and out. Concentrating on that and not on her stomach trying to come up.

"Suzanne?" Another male voice. Not John. She risked looking up and almost regretted it. Any movement made her stomach swoop.

Tyler Morrison. Everyone but her friend Claire called him Bud. He looked like a Bud. Tall and powerfully built, with light brown hair and light brown eyes which turned soft whenever he looked at Claire. His eyes were hard now, all business.

"Hi, Bud."

"You okay?"

"Peachy," she gasped and swallowed again. Her stomach seemed to have lodged itself somewhere in the middle of her chest but at least it wasn't sliding greasily upwards. She was released and a moment later John took her hand, wrapping it around a glass. "Here, drink this."

Suzanne gulped the ice water down gratefully. It went down in one chill rush, soothing the overheated feeling that accompanies a wave of nausea. "Thanks," she murmured. She tried on a smile for John but got no answering smile back. "I needed that." She turned to Bud. "You got here quickly."

"It's our new citizen-friendly policy. We aim to please." Bud smiled faintly but it was clear that he was here as 'The Police' and not as her friend Claire's boyfriend, a man she'd had drinks and dinner with. His face was serious, his manner sober. "Okay, honey. There are some things we need to go over. But before we do, I need you to do something for me. Come over here."

He gestured and Suzanne followed him to the dead body lying on his stomach. She had to step around the pool of blood and felt saliva fill her mouth. With an enormous effort, Suzanne willed her stomach to stay right where it was. John's arm slipped around her waist. She leaned into him, into the strength and the heat of him. At that moment, she didn't care what Bud thought. She was just grateful for the support of that iron arm. Her legs were shaking and she knew he would keep her upright forever, if need be.

Three men were kneeling around the body. All three had carefully chosen the few places that weren't spattered with blood. One was finishing up taking fingerprints using a curved implement she remembered seeing on CSI, another was taking swabs, and the third was using tweezers to pick up fibers, putting them in a glassine envelope.

A bright flash behind her went off and Suzanne jumped.

"Steady," John murmured, his deep voice a bare whisper, for her ears only.

She drew in a deep breath and nodded. John's arm tightened around her. They were standing hip to hip but his attention was directed outwards. His face was remote; gaze cold and vigilant as it made its way in regular sweeps around the room. Were it not for his arm firmly about her, Suzanne would have imagined that he wasn't even aware of her presence. And yet he knew every move she made.

Another flash went off, then another and another as the photographer, a short, sandy-haired man with a blond handlebar moustache, circled the body. The flashes continued steadily until finally the camera was dropped, allowed to rest hanging against the technician's chest by a leather strap.

"That about wraps it up, Lieutenant," the photographer said, stepping back.

"Okay, Lou," Bud said. "Stand by. We're going to see who we've got here."

Pulling on a pair of latex gloves, Bud kneeled on a clear patch of floor. He studied the back of dead man for a long moment. He reached out and pulled at the man's left shoulder steadily until the dead man flopped over and settled on his back.

"Okay, now." Bud sat back on his haunches. "Who is he?" he asked, looking up at Suzanne then over at John.

She steeled herself and looked down.

The dead man had a long, narrow, deeply tanned face with regular features. Without the rictus of a painful death, he might have been mildly good-looking, though it was hard to tell. The wide-open eyes were a muddy brown, starred with deep lines in the skin around them, more a result of the effects of sun and weather than age. He had crooked, yellowish teeth. One eyetooth overlapped the incisor. The hair was dark brown, straight, shot through with a few gray hairs.

Bud was watching her. "Suzanne?"

She stared for another two minutes, nauseated, and then shook her head. "I've never seen that man before in my life," she said firmly.

"John?"

John had only glanced at the dead man, and then had returned his attention back to the room. He shook his head. "Don't know him."

Bud stood, dusting his hands. "Well, you might not know him, Suzanne, but he knows you. I need to ask you a few questions." He looked over. "You, too, John," he said, faint irony in his voice.

Suzanne didn't need to ask what kind of questions Bud had for John, not with John's knife through the dead man's throat.

"Let's take it to the couch," John said, his arm still around her. Suzanne knew he was shielding her. They couldn't see the body from the couch.

He settled her on the little couch, then sat down beside her, taking up about two thirds of it. His left arm was behind her, her right side completely up against his left. He was effectively embracing her but that felt just fine. As a matter of fact, she had to clench her fists to resist the temptation to lean more heavily into him, to let his strength surround her.

His face was set and hard. He had placed the big black pistol on the coffee table, but close to hand, the butt facing him so he could pick it up and use it immediately if necessary. Though he was sitting, she could feel the coiled tension in his big body. At regular intervals, his eyes kept quartering the room, his gaze like a searchlight, only dark. She knew he had taken the measure of every person—two more technicians had joined the crime scene squad technicians milling around—and every object in the room. Something told her he was aware at all times of the position of every person and every object. And of her.

He might protect her, but he wasn't going to comfort her. He was as remote and as untouchable—except in the most physical sense of the term—as someone on the moon. And yet he kept within touching distance of her at all times.

Bud sat down across from her, looking at her somberly, then he looked over to John. He pulled out a notebook.

"Okay, want to tell me what went on?"

John turned to her. You first, his look said.

Okay.

She ran a hand through her hair. It was still a little tangled, the quick swipe with the brush she'd allowed herself in the bathroom not enough make it smooth. She'd managed to wash her face and brush her teeth, though, which made her feel better. She put her hand down to straighten up and encountered iron-hard male flesh. John's thigh. She snatched her hand away, only to find it caught in his.

His palm was hard, callused, his fingers curled tightly around hers. She didn't pull her hand away, surprised at the comfort in that single touch.

Bud noted her hand in John's but didn't say anything. He looked at her expectantly. "Where do I start?" Suzanne asked.

"Why don't we take it from when you came home last night? What did you do?" Bud looked at her expectantly and she felt a spurt of panic swell up in her chest. He wanted to know about last night?

"Last night?" she breathed, shocked.

Oh God, she couldn't talk about it. The heat and the sex. Not in front of Bud. And how on earth could Bud know she and John had—

Oh.

It was after midnight. By last night, Bud meant a few hours ago. He didn't mean—tell me about you and John and the wall. He meant—tell me about you and the dead man. Which was almost easier than the sex.

"Tell me about your day. Did you notice anyone following you? Anything unusual happen?"

"No, of course not." Anyone following her? What a ludicrous idea. She started to shake her head then thought about it. She'd entered a new world, one in which she didn't know the rules and had no survival instincts. In this new world, anything could happen. "I mean," she corrected, looking at Bud and John, "maybe someone was, but I didn't notice it. I probably wouldn't. I guess I don't think that way. But if anyone was following me, he had a very boring day. I met with a cloth importer, Cathy Lorenzetti, at nine o'clock in her office on Glisan. At ten I met with a colleague, Todd Armstrong, at his home. We had tea and discussed business. I spent the afternoon with a new client, going over the plans for the redecoration of her apartment. Not exactly the stuff thrillers are made of."

Bud absorbed this information, making careful notes. "I'm going to be needing addresses and phone numbers." Suzanne gave them to him. "And you got home around when?"

"Eight. It had been a long afternoon." Very long, Suzanne thought. And tedious. "I was tired. I took a bath, had a light meal and turned into bed."

"That would be around what time?" Bud asked. He was taking copious notes, though she couldn't imagine she was saying anything of any importance.

"Ten o'clock. I checked my watch and I remember hearing the grandfather clock—the one over there in the corner—chime ten." Bud turned around to look where she pointed and nodded. "I read for about twenty minutes, then turned out the light. I might have dozed a little, off and on, but I was feeling restless." Suzanne could almost feel John's intense scrutiny beside her. He seemed to be listening to her with every cell in his body. Surely he must know he was a big reason she'd been unable to fall asleep. "Then I heard the clock chime midnight and I realized that I was having trouble falling asleep so maybe I should heat up some milk."

"You had to walk through this room to get to the kitchen, right?" Bud gestured with his head.

"Yes. The house is a little odd in the layout because it was originally a factory. Industrial spaces are laid out quite differently from residential spaces. A residential space is divided up into day areas and night areas but this one isn't. Essentially, my apartment is four large rooms, one after the other. My office first, the public space, and then the private spaces: the kitchen, the living room and the bedroom. The bedroom's through there." She pointed, shivering inwardly at the memory of huddling in fear in the closet. John's hand tightened on hers.

It was large and hard and callused. Suzanne suddenly had a very vivid sensory memory of the hard calluses on his fingertips brushing over her breasts, brushing lower. He'd opened her roughly before plunging inside her, the calluses on his hands grating very sensitive flesh…

She turned and their eyes met and the breath left her body at the heat and power of those gunmetal dark eyes. He was remembering, too.

"So," Bud prodded, not looking up from his notes. "Let's see if I got it straight. You can't sleep, so you get up and go to the kitchen—"

With difficulty, Suzanne wrenched her attention away from John. She struggled to concentrate. "Yes. Well, no. First I went to the window in my bedroom, just for a second. It was snowing, very lightly. I love it when it does that, just a few fat snowflakes falling down. It was what I call an aurora borealis night—you know, when the clouds are low enough to reflect the lights from downtown?"

Bud nodded but John looked blank. Well, he wasn't from Portland. Apparently he wasn't from anywhere in particular. Though he must have spent some time in the south. There'd been a faint southern inflection in his voice, whispering in her ear as he thrust hard and fast inside her. She bit her lips. She couldn't be thinking about this now.

"Suzanne?" Bud was looking at her oddly. Thank God he wasn't a mind reader. "Go on."

She couldn't talk and think of John at the same time. She turned to look at Bud, like spot focusing while dancing. "So I was watching the lights reflected off the clouds when I realized that I was seeing other lights. Or rather a light. A focused one, flickering off the hedges. I watched it for a while, and couldn't understand what it was."

Bud rose and gazed out the window, measuring, then looked back at John when he sat down again. "A flashlight," he said.

"From the office," John confirmed.

Suzanne looked from one to the other. "Yes, you're right." How annoying. It had taken her at least ten minutes peering outside the window, puzzled, to reach that conclusion. "So I decided to go check to see—"

"Jesus, Suzanne," Bud said, half rising out of his seat.

"You fucking what?" John roared, outraged. His hand crushed hers in a hard grip. "You're looking at the flashlight of an intruder and you fucking go check it out! What the hell's the matter with you, lady?"

Suzanne recoiled. It was the first time she'd heard him use what probably was a sailor's vocabulary. She wasn't used to being spoken to like that. She tried to jerk her hand out from his, but he held on tight. There was no breaking that grip, no getting away.

She wanted to be indignant, to respond icily to both Bud and John—John especially—but the truth was they were right. She hadn't thought her actions through. Like last night—no, like the night before last—when John had lectured her on what she needed to secure the building.

Her mind simply didn't run along those tracks.

Bud was scowling heavily now. "That's the dumbest thing I ever heard and I've heard a lot in my time. You realize you might have an intruder in the house and you amble on over to see what he's doing?" His deep voice was heavy with disapproval as he wrote in his pad. "Do you realize how reckless that is?"

Suzanne refrained from rolling her eyes. "Well, that's not quite what happened, so you don't need to raise your voice. I went to investigate what the light source was. Not having yet reached the conclusion that I had an intruder in the house like some lightning-swift people I know."

Irony was lost on them. Bud was writing busily and John had released her hand to rise from the couch, gun in hand, and look outside the windows. He pulled back the curtains and peered intently out from first one window then the other. His broad shoulders blocked the entire window out. He stood watch for a moment, silent and motionless, then checked the door to the kitchen, the door to the bedroom. At each movement, he checked back at her as well, as if in the space of a few seconds she could disappear or someone could leap out from behind the couch to steal her away. He moved swiftly, silently, like a panther pacing the perimeter of a cage. When he returned to the couch, he placed the gun quietly back on the table, within reach. He placed his left arm again around the back of the couch, only this time he cupped her shoulder.

"Did you switch on the lights?" Bud asked.

"No," Suzanne replied. She was suddenly struck by the idea that that might have saved her life. The intruder would have come after her immediately. "Good Lord, if I had—" She couldn't finish the sentence.

"It would be your blood spatters the crime scene unit would be studying right now instead of his." John finished the sentence for her, his grip almost painfully tight on her shoulder. There were pale lines of some strong emotion—anger?—around his mouth.

Suzanne drew in a shocked breath. Her mind reeled at how close it had been. She remembered the intense feelings in the closet. How fiercely she wanted to live.

So close. She'd come so close to dying. A movement of her fingers, a flick of the light switch, and it would have been over. The blood drained from her face as she thought of what the intruder's gun could have done to her.

Both Bud and John were watching her carefully. The low murmurs of the techs working the body drifted up. She felt foolish, and tired and completely out of her depth.

"Go on," Bud said finally.

"Okay." Suzanne bit her lip. "Okay, um, I walked through the living room, this room, and into the kitchen. I heard this noise. Like a—a thud. Like someone bumping into furniture. That's when I realized that it was someone bumping around. In my office. The door was ajar. I peeked around the door and I saw him."

"The man lying on the floor?"

"I'm not too sure…I don't think I could swear to that in court." For the first time it occurred to Suzanne that she probably would be testifying in court. A murder had been committed in her home. In self-defense, to be sure, but it was still a murder. Or would that be manslaughter?

John had come running to her rescue and had killed the man. Would there be legal consequences for him? He was just starting out in a new business. Had her problems reached out to blight his life?

"I can swear that he was wearing a black leather jacket and tan pants exactly like what the dead man is wearing. He had a big gun with a barrel on the end of it. It looked like the silencers they show in the movies. He walked several times in front of the window and I could see him and the gun silhouetted against the light. But I didn't get a good look at his face. He was stumbling around a lot, looking at his feet. He was finding it hard to orient himself in the room. It's got an unusual layout, as I said, and it's Feng Shui."

Bud's pencil froze over the pad. John stopped his perusal of the room and turned to stare at her. The techs, two on their knees, looked up.

"It's…what?" Bud asked.

"Feng Shui." At their blank looks, she smiled. She'd taken lessons from Li Yung herself, who was Mandarin and who pronounced it 'Fang Choi'. "You probably know it as Feng Shui." Suzanne gave it the American pronunciation.

Bud put his pencil down and pinched the bridge of his nose. "Honey," he said, "you're going to have to make sense. Help me out here. What's—what was the word again?"

"Two words. Feng Shui. It means 'Wind and Water'."

Bud and John exchanged glances.

"Your house is wind and water?" Bud asked, carefully.

It was good to have something to smile about. "It's the ancient Chinese art of decorating a space to make best use of energy flows. The Chinese believe energy flows in specific directions and you arrange furniture and objects to direct that flow in beneficial ways. But it also means that furniture and objects aren't arranged in concentric boxes like in the West. The man found a footstool where he was expecting a chair, and a table where he was expecting nothing at all."

She might as well have been speaking Chinese. Bud looked at his techs, at John, then shrugged. "Okay. So you saw this guy stumbling around in the dark in your office, which is—" he hesitated, "whatever. What did you do then?"

"I went back through the rooms as quietly as I could and called John."

"Why John? Why not the police? Why not me?"

Suzanne lifted a shoulder. 'Why John' was evident in every line of John's big body, in the fiercely controlled grace of his every move. In the way he handled his gun, in the way his constant vigilance ensured nothing could surprise him. Why John was clear.

John's eyes were narrowed as he looked at her. She couldn't breathe properly while he was staring at her so intently. His hard jaw was dark with black stubble. He'd been close shaven the night they'd had dinner together. Had had sex together. He was probably one of those men who needed to shave twice a day. The beard made him look even more disreputable, even more dangerous. The kind of man no one crossed.

"I thought he might be close by," she whispered. John had stopped his careful quartering of the room and was focused on her. She'd almost forgotten that feeling of being in the presence of a force of nature. Now, the focus of his intent gaze, she remembered. She remembered how alive she'd felt walking by his side, how every single person in the restaurant had faded into insignificance and how he filled her entire field of vision. She remembered the ferocity of his kisses, the power of his hands on her, his penis thrusting hot and hard inside her.

She also remembered that fierce moment in the closet, one of those defining moments in a person's life. That moment the plane plunges, the car slides out of control, the earth shakes. That clear cool view of life as you might be dying.

In that moment, she'd wanted John Huntington by her side with every fiber of her being.

In that moment she'd known that he would come for her without question and that he would die for her.

In that moment, she knew that in some primal way, more a matter of blood and bone than mind and heart, she was his.

"I punched in the alarm code, like you told me," she said to John. "Honest. I remember doing it when I came home. I don't know how he got in."

"Whoa." Bud stared at John. He shook his head. "I don't believe this. That guy got past your security? Tell me it's not true. You're slipping, Midnight Man."

"Not my security," John answered tightly. "I was going to install my system tomorrow. She had Interloc."

"Okay. *Whew*. For a minute there I thought you'd lost your touch." Bud scribbled some more then looked up. "What then, honey?"

Suzanne pushed her hair wearily out of her eyes. God, she was tired. She was on her second night without sleep. "I got in touch with John. Called him on my cell phone. He said he was a few blocks away. He said to lock the doors, and to go to my closet and wait." Eyes closed, she remembered those moments, filled with panic and fear. "So I did."

Bud turned. "John?"

His eyes were dark and cold. His voice even. "I got the call from Suzanne at seventeen minutes past midnight. She said she'd seen an intruder in the house, that he was armed. I was a few blocks away. I parked out of view of the building and proceeded to the front door. The alarm system and phone lines had been disabled. I entered the building—"

"Were you armed at the time?" Bud asked sharply.

John's eyes glittered like ice. He just looked at Bud.

"Okay, okay." Bud said. "With what?"

"Sig Sauer."

"Why didn't you use it?"

"In the end, I opted not to." John shrugged a broad shoulder. "I thought he might be wearing body armor. Which he was. My weapon would have blown his face away. If his prints weren't on file, we'd never know who he was. I used my K-Bar."

Suzanne could just imagine the scene. The dark, silent room, John moving like a ghost, his big knife whipping through the air, the intruder clutching his throat, crumpling to the ground, wheezing uselessly for air while his blood pulsed and sprayed…

Bud sighed. He was sitting in male mode—legs spread wide, hands on knees, pen and pad dangling from one big hand. He sighed again, slapped his thighs and stood up.

"Okay. Let's take this down to the station house." He gestured to the technicians. Two unfolded a gurney and lifted the dead man on to it. He spoke to them. "You guys got everything?" They nodded.

John put his hand to Suzanne's elbow and helped her out of the couch. He held her thick quilted jacket. Suzanne fitted her arms into it and he lifted her hair at the back for her. His hands—heavy, warm, reassuring—lay on her shoulders while she zipped the jacket up. For just a second, Suzanne allowed herself to lean back against him a little, savoring the strength and steadiness of him.

John squeezed her shoulders gently, and then lifted his hands. "Get your things," he said quietly.

She made a wide circle around the bloodstains on the floor and wheeled her little suitcase out. Bud lifted an eyebrow and John shook his head sharply. Don't ask, his look said.

Oddly, John didn't help her with the suitcase. It was on wheels, so it was easy for her to carry. Still, he seemed like the kind of man who wouldn't let a woman carry anything.

Then he placed his left arm around her waist, picked up his big black gun and she understood. He wanted one hand on her and one hand on his weapon.

What an odd little procession they made as they trooped outside, Suzanne thought. Bud first, Suzanne and John together, then the techs with the body, two carrying the gurney, two flanking it. Suzanne stood just outside the door, blinking. Two more police cars had joined the others haphazardly parked along her street. Their lights were flashing and she could hear the squawk and hiss of the radio. Police officers milled around, their low voices muffled in the thick night air. They were already cordoning off the house with yellow police tape.

The light snowfall had left white patches on the ground. It wasn't snowing now but the air felt heavy and damp. It would snow later, maybe at daybreak in a few hours. Suzanne lifted her head and breathed in deep, trying to dispel the smell of violent death. The oxygen helped clear her brain. She felt unreal, at the center of a scene she'd seen a thousand times on TV but never imagined would be part of her life.

She watched two technicians maneuver the gurney down the steps. The body, zipped up in a black plastic bag, shifted. One of the police officers reached out to brace it before it could slip off.

She'd never seen the dead man before. How strange that a perfect stranger should want her dead. He'd come to kill her. Instead, he was the one leaving her house in a body bag and she was standing right next to the man who'd killed him.

Suzanne looked up at John. His arm was tight around her waist, though he wasn't looking at her. He wasn't looking at anything, really. His gaze raked the street, up and down, not focusing on anything in particular, but Suzanne could tell he was intensely aware of his surroundings, of everything and everyone on her street. Then he turned to look at her and she felt caught in the beam of a searchlight. A muscle in his jaw jumped and he pulled her even more tightly towards him, turned slightly inwards, his gun hand free.

She stared up at him, her breath turning white in the cold, mingling with his.

Bud came up beside her and put a hand on her shoulder. "Okay, hon," He said. "Get in the lead car and—"

"She's coming with me." John's tone was non-negotiable as he spoke to Bud over her head. "I'll drive her downtown. She's not getting out of my sight. Not for a second."

Bud stared at him and John glared back. Bud's shoulders lifted. "Okay. It doesn't make that much difference who drives her. We need to talk to you, too, anyway, as you can imagine. You know the address of headquarters?"

John nodded.

"Wait," Suzanne said. "My house." The intruder had broken her alarm system. Her building was vulnerable. "We can't just leave it like this."

John understood and squeezed her waist. "The police will post a guard. Nothing will happen to your house." He speared Bud with a hard look. "Will it?"

Bud's mouth lifted in a half smile. "Yeah, okay, sure. I can spare an agent, and of course we're putting up police tape. No one will touch your house. You'll find all your knickknacks when you get back, or Claire will have my head. It'll still be Fong—" he hesitated.

"Feng Shui." Suzanne tried to smile past her sadness. It wasn't true. Her wonderful home, which she'd labored over and dreamed about and worked on, wasn't Feng Shui any more, wasn't in tune with wind and water. The harmony of her home had been broken, the energy shattered. Her refuge had been violated. She wondered if she would ever feel safe there again.

"Right. Whatever." Bud watched the body being lifted up into a van, which had pulled up to the curb. "Let's take this down to the stationhouse. We've got a long night ahead of us." He looked up at the still-dark sky then down at his watch. It was three a.m. "Or morning. I'll lead, John. You follow me."

"This way to the car," John murmured to her once they were outside the gate. He turned left and she pulled her suitcase behind her. She felt foolish with the wheels trundling along behind her. John hadn't volunteered why he wanted her to pack a suitcase and she didn't dare ask him. Not with him so intensely focused on their surroundings. Time enough for that later.

He was scanning the empty night sky, the dark buildings, the deserted streets. But there was nothing to see. It was so late not even the streetwalker twins were out. Or maybe they were in the St. Regis, plying their trade.

As they passed by the dilapidated hotel, she wondered where John's Yukon was. He'd parked it out of sight, he said. Why couldn't they take her car? It was working like a dream now, thanks to him.

Car. She slowed. They couldn't take her car. She'd changed purses this evening and left her driver's license, together with two charge cards, on her vanity table. That wasn't good. Even if they posted an officer at the door, it wasn't smart to keep documents and credit cards out in plain sight. Not to mention the fact that she'd probably need some form of ID at the police station. Suzanne turned back.

It happened all at once.

There was a coughing sound and she felt her cheek sting. Not even a second later John slammed into her, crushing her against the wall, knocking the breath out of her. She tried to get her breath back, to ask him what he was doing, but his broad back squeezed her, hard, against the wall.

His arm lifted and she heard two loud noises, so close together it took her a second to realize there were two reports, so loud they deafened her. She was dazed, pinned against the wall, unable to see past him. She realized with a sense of shock that John had fired into a building. She peered around him, following the direction of his arm. He'd fired into the St. Regis. He'd fired a shot—no, two shots—into a hotel! Good God, he might have killed someone!

"John!" Bud shouted as he came towards them at a dead run. He reached beneath his coat and pulled out a gun as he ran. "What the hell's the matter with you, man! That's a hotel! Have you gone crazy?"

John grabbed her arm and pulled her forward, keeping himself between her and the wall. All three of them looked up at the sound of shattered glass and cracking wood. A body leaned out of the broken window frame of a second story room in the

St. Regis. It moved slowly at first, then gathered speed as it tumbled to the ground. For a second, a man had been silhouetted against the porch lights and the long deadly rifle in the man's hand was clearly visible. As was the shattered head, a mass of blood and brains.

Suzanne stood, shocked, and uttered a little cry.

"Come on." John's hand pulled at her, hard. He moved quickly and she was forced to keep pace. She slid a little on a patch of ice and he half-lifted her as he steadied her. "That was the second shooter, Bud!" he shouted over his shoulder, running and pulling her along. "Dig the bullet out of the wall if you don't believe me. You goddamned find out what's going on, you hear me, man? Until you do, you're not seeing her again!"

"Wait!" Bud yelled, his voice echoing in the empty street. "Where are you taking her?"

But John had rounded the corner at a run. Suzanne had to work at keeping up, dragging her suitcase. Shocked, shaken, she tripped. Without breaking his stride, John bent and lifted her into his arms, suitcase and all, and continued running. A block down Singer Street she could see the Yukon. He had his remote out, unlocking the doors as he ran. In just a few seconds, he'd shoved her into the passenger seat, rounded the vehicle and taken off with the sound of rubber burning.

Suzanne sobbed once, then with a shudder controlled herself. The last thing John needed at this moment was a hysterical woman. He was driving dangerously fast down the dark streets. His hands were strong on the wheel, but they were going at a speed which would be fatal if they came across another car. His eyes flicked continuously to the rear view and side view mirrors.

"Fasten your seat belt," he said, his voice calm, remote. Hands trembling, Suzanne did what he said, tucking her suitcase in the footwell so it wouldn't bounce around.

He gunned through an intersection.

"Hold on tight," he said coolly, hitting the brakes and twisting the steering wheel. Suzanne was thrown violently to the right, held in place only by the seat belt. She bit her lip to keep from screaming as they went into a long skid. She braced herself for the crash, which never came. The squeal of the tires was loud in the silence of the night and the smell of burning rubber drifted into the cab. It was clear, however, that John was in perfect control of the vehicle as he fought the wheel, pumping the brakes in a smooth rhythmic progression. He brought the SUV around facing the direction they'd come in, executing a 180° turn in a matter of seconds, and accelerated back down the street.

She'd never seen driving like that before, where the driver was an extension of the vehicle. John's gaze went from the street ahead, to the rear view mirror to the side mirror, in regular sweeps. She had to brace herself against the door as he raced through the streets, taking corners in tight turns.

"Is anyone following us?" Suzanne was proud that her voice was steady.

"No, we're clear," John replied, eyes searching the road ahead. His deep voice was remote, dispassionate. He could have been reporting on the weather—it's stopped raining now, instead of no killers are following us.

He had slowed down a little, driving steadily towards the outskirts of the city, finally passing the city limits. There were no streetlights this far from town and his face was illuminated only by the lights on the dashboard. They highlighted the rigid line of the jaw, the brutal slash of cheekbones, the strong brow.

He'd killed two men tonight. He'd done it defending her, but he had two deaths on his hands, nonetheless. He was a warrior; it was part of what he did. Suzanne had no idea how many other men he'd killed, but something about the lethal air he carried with him like an aura told her that there had been others.

She was alone in a car with a man who could kill. Who had killed. Who—if her reading of his vigilance was correct—was perfectly prepared to kill again. She had only the faintest glimmerings of who and what he was, but he was something so far outside her normal life he might as well have been a Martian who had landed in a space ship.

Yet as removed from her as he was, he was the person she'd instinctively turned to in trouble. It was as if the sex they'd had—fast and furious and rough—had somehow forged a bond that was bone deep.

Modern-day sex was supposed to be light-hearted, with no consequences if you took precautions, though she winced at the thought that they hadn't taken precautions. Still, this was the 21st century, and two unattached adults should have been able to have sex casually. Casual, mutually pleasing sex.

Sex with John had been nothing at all like that. It had been earth shattering, so intense she thought she would faint while climaxing. She'd barely slept since then and had hardly eaten. That wasn't at all what modern sex was about. Modern sex was about flirting and keeping it cool.

Not something so primitive it seemed to have come from the dawn of mankind, where men clubbed women and dragged them to their lair, then protected them with bared teeth and claws.

Some primitive instinct told her that in calling John to come to her aid, she'd crossed a dangerous, invisible line. She'd given herself over to his care. She'd given herself over to him.

Something important had changed; some turning point in her life had come. She was too shocked, too scared to follow through the ramifications of everything that had happened, but one thing was clear. She was now in John Huntington's hands. In the hands of a man she knew nothing about, save that he could kill. Easily and without remorse.

Suzanne looked at his hard profile and shivered.

A few seconds later, he pulled to the side of the road.

They had been traveling down it for over half an hour. It was deserted and unfamiliar. The last car they passed had been five minutes ago. John got out, bent briefly over the front fender and then the back fender. In a minute or two, he was back behind the wheel, folding a soft beige blanket around her.

"There you go," he said. The deep voice was low, almost gentle. Suzanne stared into his dark fathomless eyes for a long moment. Holding her gaze, he wiped her cheek with a clean handkerchief he took out of his pocket. It came away stained with blood. With a start of surprise, she realized that she'd been cut. By a shard spinning away from the wall, propelled by the force of the bullet. She hadn't felt it up until now, probably shock had dulled her senses, but now her cheek stung.

Wonderful. If she could feel the sting of pain, it meant she was alive.

"Thank you," she whispered, meaning more than for the blanket and the handkerchief. He nodded and started the engine. The heat was on full blast, but she huddled gratefully in the blanket, chilled to the bone from shock and sleeplessness. They drove on, endlessly.

Suzanne was quiet, lulled by the dark empty road. They started climbing and she stirred in the darkness.

"Where are we going?" she asked quietly.

John looked at her briefly then turned his attention back to the road.

"Where no one will ever find you," he said.

Chapter Eight

Suzanne awoke with a jolt, dry-mouthed and dazed, as the Yukon took the last of a series of hairpin turns and rocked to a stop. She sat up, banging her elbow against the door, disoriented, pushing her hair out of her eyes. She had no idea how long she'd dozed or even what time it was. Her watch was back in the bedroom, together with her lost serenity and the broken bits of what had once been her life.

All gone.

She was too tired to think coherently, but she didn't need logic to tell her that her entire existence had been ripped to shreds. Her home—her sanctuary, her refuge—was no longer safe. She'd had to abandon it in the middle of the night. Someone had come in the heart of the night to kill her and she had no idea who, and no idea why.

Until she knew, until she could be sure the nameless, faceless threat was gone, there was no going back.

Her life was shattered, wiped out in a few moments. There was no past, no future. However hard she tried, she couldn't see beyond the next five minutes. There was only the here and the now.

She'd dozed fitfully in the Yukon, the result more of exhaustion and overload than sleepiness. Something inside her balked at the idea of giving herself over to the unconsciousness of deep sleep, so she'd drowsed off and on, half-drugged with fear and shock, completely adrift as John drove the Yukon over unfamiliar roads.

Where were they? She had no idea, except probably high in the mountains. They'd been climbing steadily for hours. The sky was the pearly gray of cold mornings; light enough to see by but not enough to allow perspective.

A shack lay a few yards ahead. A simple wooden structure, square and unwelcoming. John killed the engine, plunging them into an eerie silence.

John turned in his seat, wide shoulders blocking the view of the sky out his window. "We're here." His voice was low and calm.

He seemed so huge in the cab of the vehicle, one strong arm draped over the wheel, big hand dangling. She tried and failed to wipe the image of the intruder with John's knife through his throat from her mind. The sprays of blood on the floor and the walls, the lingering smell of coppery blood and fetid death. The sound of the crackling glass as the sniper fell to his death with two bullets through his head and the wet thump as he landed. No matter how hard she tried, the sights and sounds stayed front and center of her mind, jarring, shocking.

John moved and the hairs on the nape of her neck rose, but he was only shifting to open the door. He jumped lightly down and came around to open her door. He reached for her, big hands up. She leaned forward, bracing her hands on his shoulders, feeling the banked strength there as he eased her down. Her feet touched the ground, but she kept her hands on him for a moment longer, anchoring herself to the only solid thing in a world gone suddenly insane.

They stared at each other, white breaths mingling in the cold morning air. He moved his head towards the shack. "Come on. It's too cold to stay out here. We need to get you settled in." He picked up her suitcase with one hand and took her elbow with the other.

Yes, they were in the mountains, she thought, as they tramped up the makeshift driveway full of loose gravel. The air felt thin and clean and brittle, laced with the unmistakable tang of miles and miles of uninterrupted pine trees. The few inches of snow on the ground looked like ice. They stepped up to a wooden porch. John opened the front door and gestured her inside.

Small, austere, unadorned. A sofa, two mismatched armchairs, a dining table, a small clean hearth, and a kitchenette. Bare wooden walls. Spare, cold, bleak. A musty smell permeated the shack.

"This way," John said and opened a door. It gave onto a bedroom, as spare as the other room. Just a bed and a rocking chair. He dropped her suitcase on the floor and gestured to a door to the left. "Bathroom's through there. I suggest you wash up and change into your nightgown. You must be tired and I think a few hours' sleep in a bed would do you good. Come out when you're ready. I'll turn the heat on and make you some tea."

He disappeared and Suzanne lifted her case onto the bed. Luckily, some instinct had made her pack two high-necked flannel nightgowns. They were warm and comfortable and above all, not revealing. She liked frilly sexy silk nightgowns, but now was definitely not the time for frills or silk. Or sex.

She felt raw enough as it was, on the run and alone with this large, dangerous man. Fleeing from some unknown, unseen danger.

She knew John wouldn't force himself into her bed, but she'd proved to herself the other night that she had a fatal weakness for this man. If he asked, she'd say yes. She was cold from the bones out and sex with John was guaranteed to warm her up, take her out of herself, make her forget. She'd climaxed in an explosion of heat the other night. Kissing John, feeling his hard body against hers, in hers, oh yes, that was guaranteed to make her forget her troubles. But sex right now, when she felt so shaky, so unsettled, would be disastrous.

She'd nearly come apart at the explosive orgasm, leaving her weak and out of control. She'd fly into a million pieces now that the shards of her life lay in a heap at her feet.

A muffled whump told her that he'd switched on the heating. By the time she'd used the bathroom, scrubbed her face clean, brushed her teeth and changed into her pink flannel nightgown, the air was already starting to heat up. Good. She needed the warmth.

He was sitting at the table, two steaming mugs of dark liquid before him. He looked her quickly up and down, seemingly satisfied with what he saw, and pushed a mug over to her. "Drink. Then we'll talk."

Suzanne picked it up, nose wrinkling at the smell. She took a sip and coughed, eyes watering. "Is there any tea at all in this whiskey?"

His mouth lifted in a half smile. "Very little," he confessed. "Tea is for wusses."

Must be, because there wasn't much in her cup. Suzanne sipped again and found on the second try that the hot tea-flavored whiskey went down like a dream, warming her all the way down, curling into her stomach and chasing the coldness away.

The warmth kick-started her brain. She looked around the bleak, sad, little room, then back at John. He'd abandoned the teacup and was drinking his whiskey straight, from a glass. That was a good sign. John struck her as the kind of man who would never drink alcohol if he felt danger was imminent, but she wanted to be certain.

"Where are we?"

"Near Mount Hood. The closest town is Fork in the Road, about three miles away."

Fork in the Road. The name was familiar. She had a vague memory of someone mentioning it at a cocktail party, laughing as he described it, some dinky one-horse town.

She looked down into her mug for a moment, the tea muddy and unclear. Like her life. "Are we safe?" she asked quietly.

He drained the glass, never taking his eyes off her. "Safe? Yeah." He poured another finger of whiskey into her mug and gestured for her to drink it, waiting until she'd choked it down. "Absolutely. To find us, they'd have to look for me, but I don't think anybody besides Bud knows we're connected. Unless you checked me out with anyone else on that list I gave you?" He raised an eyebrow.

"No," she sighed, "I didn't. Bud's word was enough."

"Remind me when all this is over to chew you out for that. You should have checked me out with everyone, but given the circumstances, I'm glad you didn't."

"Unlike you, I'm not constantly on the lookout for danger," Suzanne said dryly.

"Yeah, well, if you'd been more like me then maybe we wouldn't be in this mess in the first place."

Suzanne opened her mouth then closed it, appalled. What was there to say? He was right.

"Sorry," he muttered, a muscle jumping in his jaw. "That was way out of line." He poured himself another shot of whiskey and drank it in one swallow, like water. "So let's get back to risk assessment. Nobody knows you're with me. We hadn't signed the lease yet and anyway I'm going to make sure Bud won't let anyone in the house to go through our stuff, get my name. I'm almost certain there were only two killers. That's standard procedure when you want to wipe your tracks. The second shooter's there to kill the first and erase the connection.

"I parked well out of sight of your street, but just in case the second shooter managed to notice my vehicle and called it in to whoever his boss is, I changed the license plate numbers. And I made damned sure nobody was following us."

She blinked. "You changed…what?"

John shrugged. "I keep several spare sets of plates in the back. They come in handy from time to time. "

"But isn't that illegal? Driving with false license plates?"

He shrugged again, not even bothering to answer.

"I own all the land for several miles around," he continued. "The land is registered in the name of a shell company. It would take a very determined and very skillful person several weeks to get to my name, assuming he knew what he was looking for. And even then, I hacked into the land register and changed the data, so they'd be looking fifty miles west, in a state park. The perimeter's got trip wires and I know whenever anything bigger than a rabbit gets through. So yes," he concluded. "We're as safe as we'll ever be. We could probably stay holed up here forever, though I'm counting on finding out what's going on before that."

Suzanne just stared and stared, feeling more than ever as if she'd stepped into an alternate universe. And yet, deep inside herself she knew.

She hadn't, like Alice, fallen down a rabbit hole. This wasn't an alternate world. It was this world, as it really is, as it has always been. Dirty and dangerous and violent. She'd spent her entire lifetime avoiding this reality, steeping herself in pretty things, fretting over colors and shapes and textures, maybe in an effort not to think about what the world was really like.

Look what it had got her, hiding her head in the sand. Pretty, perfumed sand, taupe and ecru, but sand all the same, and her head sunk way down in it.

She hadn't seen danger coming at all.

It was entirely possible that if she'd taken just half the care in installing a proper security system in the building that she'd taken with the color scheme, none of this would have happened. There wouldn't have been an intruder. She wouldn't be here—wherever here was—holed up, hiding from God knows what and God knows who, having endangered the life of a good man and dragged him away from his growing business.

He'd come running to her rescue without hesitation and if he hadn't been so skilled, it would have been his blood staining her hardwood floor, his head a bloody pulp. Now he was here with her, and plainly he was planning on staying with her for as long as it took. How long until Bud was able to figure out what was going on?

Days? Weeks? Months? Years maybe?

What had she done? Her throat closed tight with guilt and sorrow.

She put her mug down with a clatter. "I'm so sorry," she whispered, unshed tears burning in her eyes.

He was sipping from his glass. He swallowed heavily, coughed. "What? You're sorry? What the hell for?" He looked genuinely astonished, which made her feel even worse.

Suzanne bit her lip. I will not cry, I will not cry. "I'm sorry for involving you in this mess, John. And I don't even know what the mess is. I'm sorry for endangering your life, I'm sorry you had to kill someone—two someones—for me. I'm sorry if you're going to have trouble with the law because of what you did for me. I'm sorry…"

"Whoa. Wait a second." He held up a large-palmed hand and frowned. "You're not making sense here."

"I'm sorry I wasn't any help to you. I've always meant to take self-defense courses but I never got around to it, and if you want to know the truth, I am a total wimp. I can't even face up to Murphy the garage owner jerk and by the way, I never thanked you for picking up my car. I'm sorry you had to deal with Murphy for me, that's never pleasant. I'm sorry I didn't know how to do anything but cower in a closet," she continued, past the huge lump in her throat. "I'm sorry I wasn't able to defend myself and had to call in the Marines. Literally." She gave a choked laugh, cutting it off before it could become a sob. "I'm so sorry I forced you into hiding, sorry you have to stay holed up here with me, sorry…just…sorry." She covered her face with trembling hands. She was flying apart, shaking, taking deep breaths to hold herself together.

"Fuck this," John snarled, pushing back his chair so hard it fell to the dusty wooden floor with a clatter, and scooped her up. He held her high in his arms, moving quickly into the bedroom.

He didn't switch on the light. Just sat down on the chair, holding her, and began to rock.

Suzanne turned her face to his neck, no longer bothering to fight the tears, which welled out of her. He held her in silence, tightly, probably realizing that she didn't need words at all. She needed this, human contact, human warmth. A connection however tenuous with his strength and courage.

One large hand covered the back of her head, another held her tightly around the waist and it was as if she had permission to let it all go. Throughout it all John simply held her so tightly she could feel his chest lifting and falling with his deep, even breathing. She could hear, even feel, the slow steady heartbeats, steady and strong just like he was and it gradually calmed her.

When the bout ended, she felt dazed and exhausted. Fatigue and whiskey had demolished her defenses. She couldn't have moved if her life depended on it.

Her arms were tightly wound around his neck. If she was choking him, he wasn't complaining. Maybe he was uncomfortable sitting there with her on his lap but he didn't say anything, just held her close. How much time had gone by? She had no idea. She stirred, trying to muster the energy to get up, but his arm tightened and she slumped back against him.

Her hip came up against his erection, huge and hard and she quivered. She remembered every second of his penis inside her, how he'd thrust with the whole strength of his body, how she'd flown apart.

He wasn't thrusting up against her in sexual demand, but he wasn't hiding it either. It was there—he was aroused but he wasn't pushing for sex.

Oh God, she couldn't deal with any of this. Sex and death. Death and sex. It was too much. Her body simply gave up the fight. Sleep was falling as swiftly as night in the tropics. But before she fell asleep in his arms, there was something he had to know.

"I'm glad you were there," she whispered against his neck, her lips moving across the skin in what was almost a kiss.

"So am I," he whispered back.

Chapter Nine

She'd fallen asleep like a child, from one breath to the next, John thought. He himself didn't have any experience with children, but that's what his married buddies always told him. Kids could drop off to sleep in an instant, just like that, they said.

Except Suzanne was no child. His raging hard-on was very clear on that.

She thought that she could hide herself from him inside a high-necked flannel nightgown, but hell, she couldn't hide inside a burlap bag. She'd still be totally desirable. High-necked the gown might have been, but the shape of her breasts—her braless breasts—was clearly visible, the tight little nipples outlined against the pretty pink fabric. It was the cold making her nipples hard, not thoughts of having sex with him. So he managed—barely-—to keep from tossing her onto the bed, ripping the nightgown in two and crawling on top of her. Opening her with his fingers and sliding his cock right in.

He knew exactly what being inside her felt like and he wanted more. Right now.

Part of it was his obsession with her, that ice princess air she had which contrasted so sharply with the curvy femininity, the luscious, slightly overlarge mouth, perfect creamy skin, large, slightly uptilted eyes…

But part of it was adrenaline. He was coming down from a firefight and extraction and that always made him hard as a rock.

It was an aspect of soldiering that didn't figure in Hollywood movies or Tom Clancy novels. Movies showed men smoking, laughing, high-fiving each other after battle, but the truth was that men after battle were strung out, grim, tense and shaking, sporting woodies as hard as rocks. Willing to fuck a knothole in the wall to get it out of their system.

Every soldier in the world knew it, knew that surviving a fight required sex afterwards—hard and fast and furious—to bleed off the tension. A barracks after a takedown was so filled with testosterone you could smell it, it fogged the air so much. Soldiers had hard-ons after fights and that was a fact of life. Some would get it on with a female goat if a woman wasn't around, but he'd always drawn the line at anything kinky. If a semi-attractive and willing woman wasn't available, his fist worked just fine.

He had a more than semi-attractive woman in his arms right now and his hips surged upwards reflexively as his cock, all on its own, sought to enter her. She was right there, legs across his lap, ass right over his cock. Through the nightgown he could feel the little scrap of material over her hip. Probably a copy of those incredibly sexy little lace panties he'd ripped off her the other night, in his frantic haste to get inside her. Right now, right now, goddamn it, he could pull the soft flannel up, rip her panties off again—he'd have to start buying her underwear by the ton—spread her legs until she straddled him and thrust right up into her, and she'd be sweet and tight and smooth and all his…

Jesus.

He remembered every second his cock had been in her, everything about it. The tightness, the heat, the wetness…she'd been thinking about sex just as much as he had over dinner.

Suzanne sighed in her sleep, shifting slightly, slithering over his cock. He froze. Sweat broke out on his face, though there was still a slight chill in the air the heating system hadn't managed to dispel.

A good soldier visualized, running what he wanted to do through his head until he could see and feel the moves, until the moves were second nature, running a successful future battle through his mind so many times that by the time the real thing rolled around, the op went down smooth as ice.

John was damned good at visualizing, at projecting himself forward in time to an op, going over the details again and again. It wasn't something he could turn off, just like he couldn't turn off his ability to prepare for future danger or countering danger when he met it.

Right now he was visualizing like crazy. Visualizing doing all the things to her he hadn't had time to do the other night because he'd been nearly half-crazy with lust. Not that he wasn't in the same state right now. There had to be some point in the future in which he was going to be able to make love to Suzanne Barron instead of fucking her blind. When he'd had her enough times to assuage this burning hunger, when he'd come inside her often enough that he could savor the feel of her instead of craving it…then maybe he'd settle down some.

Maybe.

But he'd already been too rough the other night and that was without post-fight adrenaline raging through his system. Now he suspected he'd hurt her. Enter her too quickly, thrust too hard, Jesus maybe even bite her.

That thought made him back down a little.

Some women liked rough sex. John knew that for a fact and he'd had his share of them. Women who bit and scratched, who didn't mind being sore afterwards. Who got off on barely-controlled violence.

That wasn't Suzanne. She'd been shocked the other night at the roughness, though maybe she'd been shocked at her reaction, too. And what a reaction. He remembered every ripple of her sheath contracting sharply around his cock. Her excited pants, the dilated pupils.

No, he might have made her come, explosively even, but rough sex wasn't her thing.

And right now he wasn't capable of anything but rough sex.

He wasn't the only one coming down off an adrenaline high. She'd shown clear signs of it with the desperate, frantic apologies and the crying. She didn't have the right equipment for a hard-on, but tears bled out stress, too.

He looked down at her in his arms, a tear still drying on that high perfect cheekbone, crystal over purest white marble.

Jesus but the woman was gorgeous. She'd been enticing when they'd met, and he'd been blown away by the sleekly beautiful confident woman: successful, completely together, across the desk. But the woman in his arms, now—bedraggled, without makeup, eyes swollen with tears—that woman was a heartbreaker. He wanted her, every way there was.

He rose with her in his arms and curved down to put her in the bed. She barely stirred when he tucked her in and he stood for a long moment, watching her sleep. Feeling things shifting inside him, things he had no words for. The only thing he remotely recognized amongst the thousand emotions rolling inside himself was lust. He had a steel hard-on and he headed, relieved, for the bathroom because at least he knew what to do about that.

He had no frigging clue what to do about his heart but he knew exactly what to do about his cock.

Luckily he kept spare clothes up here in his mountain hideaway. He'd bought the place his second week in Portland. Just a shack with a big, insulated cellar, which was the main reason he'd got it.

He'd decorated it in exactly one extremely painful and clueless hour at the closest Wal-Mart, choosing the first pieces of furniture he'd come across, not knowing what the hell he was doing, and having three beers afterwards to calm his nerves.

He stripped, leaving his clothes with their funk of the sweat of battle on the floor and got under the shower. The water was only luke-warm but that was okay. He should have a cold shower, actually, but he was suffering enough as it was.

Here he was, naked and raring to go, Suzanne Barron was in his bed not ten feet from here and there wasn't a damned thing he could do about it. If that wasn't torture, he didn't know what was.

He dropped his hand to his groin, and remembered.

She had a little chocolate beauty spot right next to her ear. He'd licked it as he was taking her. Then he'd licked her ear and she moaned and it had been as if he'd had another gear and she'd kicked it. He'd almost doubled the speed of his strokes before the moan had finished its echo.

His heart pounded and his hand worked as he remembered every inch of her, the taste of her nipples, her tongue against his, the soft ash-brown pubic hair covering her mound. He'd done her so hard that if she shaved there as some women did, his trousers would have abraded the skin.

His fist was working hard and fast now, pumping, as he remembered her tightness, how her breath had exploded in a little puff with each thrust, how somehow halfway through she'd managed to open her legs even wider for him, how he'd clutched her perfect ass, trying to pull her closer to him, even as he was pounding into her so hard it was a miracle the wall held.

She'd screamed, her voice muffled by his coat, as she came. As John remembered in exquisite detail how he'd fucked her through her climax before exploding himself, he could feel the prickles in the backs of his legs, rising up through his spine. His cock swelled and he leaned one-handedly against the wall, weak-kneed and breathless, as he came in one long endless spurt.

He stayed under the shower for a long time, leaning against his hand, head bowed under the now-cold water thinking—I'm in deep shit.

He was in trouble—real bad trouble—if jerking off to the thought of Suzanne Barron was ten times more exciting than actually having sex with any other woman.

* * * * *

"Okay, Bud, talk to me." John leaned back in the rolling leather chair holding an untraceable cell phone to his ear.

When he'd felt his legs would hold him up—and that had taken more time than he was comfortable thinking about—he'd pulled on a black tee shirt and faded gray sweatpants and padded barefoot into the living room. Nudging aside the cheap supermarket rug, he'd reached down and put his thumb to a scanner. A blue steel panel opened up seamlessly, while a stainless steel ladder stretched down to the floor of the cellar.

As always, John felt a glow of satisfaction entering his little high-tech lair. Upstairs he sort of realized that the shack was bleak though he had no frigging clue what to do about it, but downstairs in the cellar—well, there everything was top of the line, as perfect as it could be. He'd had access to the best in the world in the Teams and damned if he was going to settle for less in civilian life.

Downstairs was his little playground, row after row of gleaming electronics, monitors, keyboards, gizmos and widgets up the ying-yang. You name it, he had it.

He'd waited until Suzanne had fallen asleep before heading down here to his spy kingdom. She was spooked enough as it was, without seeing that he had what looked like Houston Mission Control down here.

He was perfectly aware that most civilians were absolutely clueless about the dangers of the world, the big scary things out there. He'd trained for vigilance his entire life and it was now as much a part of him as breathing.

But if you weren't a soldier, if your life didn't depend on fanatic attention to detail and an underlying awareness that enemies were out there and could strike at any time, if nothing bad had ever happened to you, why then he came off as a totally paranoid freak. A number of women had been completely turned off by his constant awareness of danger, the precautions he took.

The way he wouldn't let a woman walk on the side closest to the road. Not out of chivalry but because women stupidly carried purses dangling right there off their shoulders, hanging by a thin leather strap. Big brightly colored purses screaming, "Hey! I've got money and credit cards right here!"

Why the hell did they do that? He could never figure it out. It was such a dumbass thing to do, like walking around with a bull's eye on your back. Any passing scumbag on a bike or motorcycle with a flick knife could slash and grab and that was why he walked on the outside. They'd think twice about slashing and grabbing him.

He never even paid lip service to the ridiculous notion that a woman could defend herself against a mugger; he didn't care how many self-defense courses she took and no matter what her shrink said. If she was his date for the night—even if they would never see each other again after the sex—then she was under his protection and he acted accordingly. It made a lot of women angry that he couldn't pretend the world wasn't full of predators and that nature had made women prey. So he was used to making most of his precautions as invisible as possible.

He'd been called a dinosaur often enough, not that he cared, except that it was inaccurate. Dinosaurs didn't know how to keep up with the times and he did. He knew exactly what to do and how to do it and he'd stayed alive so far under the most dangerous conditions life had been able to throw at him because of it.

Like now.

No one but Bud and the police could know Suzanne was with him. No one had followed them. Even if someone was looking for him, it would take a long time to connect this shack with him, and that included Bud and the police and all the resources they could muster.

John was good at what he did, good at arranging security. He knew the security here was about as tight as that of a nuclear power plant. Maybe tighter. They were safe as safe can be. But a good soldier always double-checks and he was still alive because he never ever took anything for granted. Ever.

So he sat down and checked his equipment.

He had the sweetest new toy and he loved it. A series of sensors with a special microchip programmed with an algorithm to detect heartbeats. And not just any heartbeat, oh no. That was the beauty of the little gizmo invented by Crazy Mac Rowan, the Team computer geek. The chip could distinguish human heartbeats from the heartbeat of 10 mammalian species by the frequency, so the alarm wasn't tripped by a deer or a bear. The system had been bought for a cool ten million dollars by the INS for use by the Border Patrol but Crazy Mac had given him the prototype. John ran his special program and found exactly what he was hoping to find.

Nada. Zip.

Next step, the motion sensors. Then the bank of monitors connected to weatherproofed cameras all around the perimeter of his land. Then the sensors along the dirt road leading up to the shack. Nothing, nothing and nothing.

No one here, no one coming. Great.

Okay. Now he could call Bud.

Bud sounded tired. "We're in trouble, John," he said. "Big time. Both guys' prints came up immediately on NCIS. First shooter's a street punk, been in and out of the cooler all his life starting from juvie when he was fourteen. Assault, rape—"

John's blood ran cold. Rape. Once a rapist always a rapist. Jesus Christ, the guy would have had Suzanne at his mercy. He would have raped her before killing her.

He was surprised his hands didn't leave prints on the phone, he was clutching it so hard.

"—armed robbery, drugs...you name it. And he was a hophead to boot, had tracks on his arms, so give him some spare cash to shoot up with and he'd have taken out a school of kids for you. We're talking walking loaded gun here, man. Pay, aim and fire. Though looks like he was the kind of weapon that can blow up in your face, flip on a dime. That's the good news. The bad news is that the second shooter was a real pro. FBI's been all over me this past hour; the Portland Special Agent in Charge is here with me right now. They had a red flag for anyone asking for his prints. They've been tracking him for 10 years. He's the prime suspect behind the assassination of Senator Lesley eight years ago. He's wanted for a couple of other big-name take-outs, too.

"Someone seriously wants Suzanne dead, big guy, and this someone's prepared to pay major bucks for it. I don't know who it is, but whoever he is, he's hired a pro, a real expensive one from what the Feebs are saying. We need to talk to Suzanne, Midnight. We need you to bring her in. Now."

Bud was crazy. The police weren't going anywhere near her. No one was.

"No way, Bud," John said coldly. "You'll see her if and when you figure out what's going on and then convince me you've figured out a way to stop it. Not before. You'll hear from me tomorrow and you'd better have some hard facts and a pretty good plan for dealing with this. And you post two men outside Suzanne's house, front and back. No one gets in."

"Hey wait, where the hell are you—" Bud said as John pressed the 'off' button. He waited grimly to get himself under control, until his breathing slowed and the red mist of rage in front of his eyes cleared.

Someone seriously wanted Suzanne dead?

They'd have to go through him first.

He headed upstairs. From now on, Suzanne wasn't going to be more than a hand-span's length from him.

* * * * *

It was late afternoon when she woke up. The sky outside the large wood-framed window was the deep blue of the evening sky at high altitude. There wasn't a cloud to be seen. The pine trees cast long blue-black shadows that told her the day was coming to an end. She'd slept the day away.

Something warm and hard gripped her hand and she slowly turned her head on the pillow, knowing what she'd see, her heart tripping a beat anyway as her eyes met John's.

Her breathing slowed and she felt calm, certain. They'd been moving towards this from the instant they'd met.

It's time, she thought.

He was sitting in the rocking chair by the head of the bed, holding her hand, watching her. Had he slept? There was no way to tell. He looked as he always looked—strong and indestructible.

He'd changed into a black tee shirt, which hugged his deep, powerful chest, stretched tightly over the huge biceps, and a pair of thin gray sweatpants grown soft with washing. She could clearly discern the massive thigh muscles.

He was hugely erect and that could be clearly seen, too. Her gaze was riveted on his groin. His penis came away from his stomach to lengthen, pulsing, and then flatten against his abdomen again.

Amazing, that she could do this to him, that she held such power. The ancient power of womanhood. The crying and the deep sleep and perhaps even the whiskey had done her good, had cleared her mind, filling it with a deep sense of certainty. She was now in another world, an ancient one, as old as man, where ties are forged in blood and iron. A world where the laws were lost in the mist of time, but no less strong for that.

They were bound by the most ancient law of all.

He had fought and killed for her. She was his.

Chapter Ten

It's time, John thought.

He had watched over Suzanne while she slept, holding her hand.

To give her comfort, because the animal part of a human knows when it's safe to let go and when it's not. It was why soldiers always post guards at night, even when there is no imminent danger. So the other soldiers can sleep at ease.

Suzanne slept deeply, giving herself over completely to unconsciousness, because at some level she knew he was there to watch over her.

But he held her hand for his own sake, too. To comfort himself. To know completely and totally that she was safe. Bud's news had shaken him to the core. The danger stalking her was real and he could lose her almost as soon as he'd found her. So he held her hand to reassure her and to reassure himself.

He wanted her more than ever.

He had to be real careful here, the desire was all tangled with a powerful drive to make her his. He couldn't let his feelings spill over into violence. Guarding her sleep was reassuring but it wasn't doing anything to slake his hunger.

His entire body was tense with lust; he was walking a thin line of control here. The powerful feelings coursing through him must have slipped his leash, edged over to her. Suzanne's breathing changed and she stirred in the bed. He watched.

Waiting. Wanting.

Suzanne eased smoothly from deep sleep to consciousness, eyes fluttering open slowly. She looked out the window at the gathering night, and then turned her head on the pillow. When her eyes met his, light to dark, it was like a punch to the stomach. He exhaled sharply, the sound loud in the silent room.

They could have been the last human beings on the planet. Just the two of them, man and woman, the oldest tie there was. She was his and she was in his cave.

His.

He reached out with his free hand to trace her mouth, the outline, where the skin turned from pink to ivory. She didn't move in any way, large gray eyes watching him, but he could feel the stir of air against his finger as she breathed.

"I don't want to hurt you," he whispered. "I was too rough the other night. I don't want to be rough."

Her eyes searched his. She didn't speak. He listened to the sound of her breathing in the quiet room. "You won't be," she murmured finally and his heart kicked its rate up.

It's time.

She knew, too. She felt it too, this rightness, this inevitability.

Don't let me mess this up. John sent up a silent prayer to whoever it was who watched over soldiers. Take it easy. Go slow.

His finger moved from her mouth to her cheekbone, tracing the fine line of it, skimming over the barely-visible scab where a shard of brick had grazed her cheek. By a miracle, the bullet had smashed into the wall, not into her.

So close. So damned close.

The skin of his hand was dark and rough against the pale smoothness of hers. He moved his hand gently over her cheekbone, letting his fingers roam. The outline of her face, a shapely oval, down over the delicate jawbone, up over her mouth again, then back down to the smooth expanse of her neck. His finger dwelled on her pulse point, feeling the slow steady beat of her heart and as his eyes rose to meet hers, he could feel the exact moment her pulse speeded up. Moving his hand down, his finger caught on the high-necked flannel nightgown and he waited, every muscle in his body clenched, his cock pulsing with anticipation.

They watched each other; John totally unsure of what he should do—what he could do—next.

Suzanne reached up with her hand and touched his, moving it aside. He wanted to howl with frustration. If she didn't want this now, he'd... but no. That wasn't it.

She'd moved his hand aside so she could unbutton the neckline herself, slowly. He watched, fascinated, as one by one she slipped the little pink and white buttons through the buttonholes, unbuttoning them all, stopping when the buttons stopped, below her breasts. She lay her hand on her stomach, watching him. Waiting.

His call.

He knew exactly what to do now. Trying not to be too eager, trying not to shake, trying hard not to—shit!—rip the cloth...

"Sorry," he muttered.

She laughed. Yes, thank you, God. That soft sound was actually a laugh. She was laughing at his clumsiness and she was right to. He chanced a smile himself. Her lips turned up in a wide smile in return.

She shook her head. "You're going to have to start buying me underwear and nightgowns if you keep this up."

Oh, yeah. "Yes," he said fervently. "Panties by the dozen, a gross of nightgowns. Yes." He opened the nightgown and went still.

"Oh, John." Her voice was a mere whisper and the smile was gone. She saw what was in his eyes as he spread the wings of the nightgown. She was laid out for him like a feast...

Pretty didn't even begin to describe it. She wasn't lushly built, like some women he'd had, who now seemed grossly overblown because this—this—was exactly what he wanted. This was what turned him on so badly he was trembling.

He just sat and stared, hoping some blood would eventually make a return journey from his cock to his brain. Opening the nightgown had been like opening an exquisite present to himself. Her smooth skin was so pale she probably never took the sun. She glowed like a pearl in the evening light, something so rare and delicate he was almost afraid to touch it.

Her breasts were round and firm, smaller than his cupped hand. He reached out and ran his finger—just the tip, so gently he was barely grazing her skin—over her right breast, following the line of a blue vein as visible as a river from a helicopter. He circled the aureole, excited as hell to see that she got goose-bumps and that the nipple turned deep rose and hard.

Take it easy, take it easy.

He just sat there for a long moment, getting his breathing under control, hand curled around her breast.

"We've got to get this thing off you." He removed his hand because otherwise he'd tear the thing off and he knew for a fact that Fork in the Road didn't run to delicate pink nightgowns. "Can you do it?"

"Okay." Watching him closely, Suzanne sat up, bunched the pink material in her hands and pulled. She wasn't wearing panties. John watched, fascinated, as the gown uncovered long, lovely legs, round hips, a tiny waist, then was pulled up over her head, tossed to the side and then yes! There she was. Naked.

Just for him.

The other night he hadn't had a chance to see all of her. He'd stripped her and entered her before her clothes had fluttered to the ground. He'd been way too far-gone to notice anything at all other than the tight, wet heat of her. But now, ah, God, now here she was. If he hadn't been hard as steel, ready to explode, he'd have spent the next couple of hours just looking and touching that soft soft skin, noticing the sharp indentation under the rib cage where her waistline narrowed, then curved out again, marveling at how delicately she was built. How did all of her organs fit inside?

He'd think about that later. Now he wanted—no, needed—to touch his mouth to her.

Leaning forward, he placed his lips on her neck, where the pulse was fluttering wildly. He could feel how the touch of his mouth excited her.

It was good to have these signs, her wild heartbeat, the fast breathing, and the hard little nipples. God knows his excitement was hugely visible.

But there was another way to see if she was as aroused as he was. He licked the pulsing vein in her neck, a long slow lap of his tongue as he moved his hand downwards. Past the soft breast, where the heartbeat could be seen and felt in her left breast, over the rib cage, across the flat little belly, down, down…

The hair here was soft, almost silky and not stiff and crinkly as most women's pubic hair was. She took the hint of his hand cupped over her mound and let her legs fall open. He slid his fingers down and around and touched her lips there. Soft, warm and yes, wet. His hand trembled as he spread the lips and inserted a finger, frowning at the difficulty and at her sudden intake of breath.

She was so goddamned tight.

He eased his finger in slowly, realizing that he must have hurt her the other night. His cock was for sure bigger than his finger. Even with his finger, he was having to enter her by degrees. The other night he'd just crashed his way in and started fucking her as if she were a ten dollar whore and he was a sailor on shore leave after a year at sea. He winced at the memory.

He pushed in further and she closed around his finger like a fist.

He withdrew his hand a little then penetrated her again, barely inside the entrance.

"You haven't fucked much, have you?" he asked hoarsely. She didn't react to his hard words. He was used to soldiers' talk—there wasn't any political correctness at all in the Teams—

but beyond that, he was too blasted by lust to look for other words, prettier ones, and softer ones. Just the blunt truth—you're so damned tight I can tell you haven't been fucked much.

"No." Her voice was low, an almost soundless whisper.

"That's changing." There was a tightness in his chest. He could barely get the words out. His voice was harsh, strained. "Starting now."

Two quick swipes of his hands and he was naked. Then he was stretching out on the bed next to her, spreading her legs wider with shaking hands. He mounted her, opened her with two fingers, positioned his cock and thrust blindly…

He stopped at her sharply indrawn breath, just an inch or two inside her. He was hard as a rock. He wanted to just plunge in so badly he was shaking with the effort to stop. But this is where he'd messed things up before. Once was bad enough. Twice and he'd lose her. He couldn't do it this way. He pulled out.

Wrapping his arms around her, he rolled them over, holding her upright with his hands.

"Oh." She looked startled, as if the idea of being on top of a man had never occurred to her before. The folds of her sex opened to ride along the base of his cock, her knees straddling his rib cage. They looked at each other and she smiled faintly. She smoothed her hands over his shoulders and clutched his biceps. "Well." She stirred a little along his cock, riding him gently up and down, testing. "This is interesting."

"Mm." He was breathless. He had no words; only heat so great he thought his head would explode. He put his hands on her waist and lifted her so she was half-kneeling.

"Stay."

Did he say that or just think it? Whatever, she understood and hovered over him, moist lips pouting between her thighs. He lifted his cock upright and positioned it under her, holding it.

His jaws clenched tight at the first brush of her sex. She slid along the head of his cock, trying to find the right position, sliding back and forth. She bore down a little, sliding forward and then yes! He was in.

Barely. She wasn't moving at all, dammit, hovering over him. Just the head of his cock was in and he was going crazy. She moved a little, circling her hips and he slid in a little further. It wasn't enough. At this rate, it would take her half an hour to slide down enough to take all of him and he didn't have half an hour.

Already he was bathed in sweat, heart hammering, breath bellowing in and out, like he'd been out on a five mile run. And they weren't even having sex yet. Not really.

Her eyes were closed and she had a dreamy expression on her face as she moved slowly. She lifted herself away and he felt like screaming with frustration, but she didn't disengage entirely. Just stayed still a moment, kneeling over him, gently moving, letting the head of his cock swirl over her lips. Then she found the right angle again and slowly moved down.

And stopped.

She was driving him nuts. Goddamit, why wouldn't she just let him in?

Teeth clenched, John held her hips and thrust upwards, hard, grinding into her.

Suzanne gasped. Her eyes opened and met his. The dreamy expression was gone, replaced by distress, maybe even pain. No, no, no! He had to make it better for her this time.

He windmilled his arms up and back. Fists clenched around the bars of the iron bedstead, he clung, shaking. He wouldn't touch her, he couldn't touch her. If he did he'd be too rough. What he wanted was to grip her hips and do her hard. Too hard.

He lay still under her, waiting for her to do something. Giving her the lead.

Suzanne stared down at him, breathing fast, fully impaled on his cock. Her pale pubic hairs meshed with his black ones. She was motionless; eyes open so wide he could see the whites around the gray-blue irises.

She rested her hands on him, feeling the deep, quick rise and fall of his chest, watching him. She seemed to him like some wary wild animal, a deer in the forest, pierced by an arrow. Watching the hunter, gauging intentions.

"Bend down to me," he whispered, clinging so tightly to the iron rods it was a miracle he didn't pull them away. He couldn't touch her with his hands, not yet. Lust was boiling inside him, slick and hot, totally uncontrollable. He had big hands, strong hands. Hands that couldn't stroke and caress. Not now. Not yet. He'd bruise her if he touched her with his hands.

She was bending down to him, close enough so he could smell the sweet warmth of her skin, rising above the smell of arousal and sex. Her hair brushed his cheek, filling his nostrils with her perfume. His jaws clenched.

"Lower." The word was guttural and came from deep within his chest. She swayed lower and his mouth opened and clamped on her nipple. She tasted sweet and salty at the same time. Smooth around the nipple, hard little bud in his mouth. He drew on her, long deep drafts of her, suckling with the strength of his mouth. His mouth worked rhythmically, hard, faster now. In time with her breathing, loud in the room. Her thighs, clamped along the sides of his chest, trembled.

She was panting, little moans coming from deep in her throat. The moans starting coming in rhythmic spurts, in time with his suckling.

Their eyes locked. He watched her eyes carefully, because there he could read what was happening to her. She was fully aroused. The pupils expanded until there was only a silver rim around them, glowing bright in the dim, failing light. He was connected to her only by his mouth around her nipple and his cock deeply embedded in her, but it was like he was touching her all over. He could feel what was happening to her body as keenly as he knew what was happening to his.

He wasn't moving and neither was she, but they were both on that knife-edge, hanging there, ready to tumble over.

She was trembling deeply, shaking all over. He sucked hard, rubbing his tongue over her pebble-hard nipple before biting lightly and suddenly she gasped.

Her cry echoed around the room, in time with the sharp contractions of her cunt around him, in time with his groans, in time—oh God!—with the spurts of his cock as he came and came and came. She was milking him dry, pulling the come out of him from what felt like his backbone.

They watched each other, trembling, motionless, until finally, after endless moments, she softened and stilled. With a soft moan, Suzanne slid bonelessly down on top of him. Her narrow rib cage rose and fell. Her head nestled into his shoulder and he could feel her breath on his skin, the flutter of her eyelashes, and the soft silk of her hair brushing against his chest.

"Wow," she whispered.

He waited until his breathing slowed, until he could control his muscles again. Slowly, he unclenched his hands from the iron bars, finger by finger, and brought them down to curve lightly around her back.

He could touch her now, finally.

Now that he'd taken the edge off.

* * * * *

Suzanne lay on John's massive chest, rising and falling with his breathing. His chest was so broad her thighs, riding along his sides, were open to their maximum extension. Somehow it wasn't uncomfortable, though she knew she'd be sore later. What did it matter? She glowed from head to toe with the aftermath of an explosive orgasm. She was surprised she hadn't been struck blind. Her body was rippling with an impossible mix of crackling energy and complete lassitude.

He was still hard inside her. How could that be? He'd climaxed, too. There was no mistaking it, that incredible feeling. He'd got harder and harder and finally just exploded. She wriggled a little, feeling the wetness filling her. She was wildly excited but that wasn't the source of the wetness. She was filled with his semen.

And yet he still felt like a rod of warm steel. Amazing. Though what was she going to do with a rock-hard penis inside her when she could barely gather the energy to breathe?

John's hands stopped running up and down her back and moved downwards to cup her backside. His hands were big, warm and rough. He pressed down as his hips flexed upwards and she gasped. He filled her to the edge of discomfort. Almost, but not quite pain. More a complete fullness.

His short hair rasped on the pillow as he turned his head and kissed her neck, then her ear. When he spoke, she could feel the vibrations more than hear the words.

"That's the way we're going to have to do it from now on, darlin'." Again, that intriguing hint of the South in his voice, low and languorous. It only came out during lovemaking. The rest of the time, his deep voice was clipped, accentless. "We've got to come first, you and me, make you all soft and wet. Now you're used to me. See? Now I can slide in and out, easy as you please."

While he was talking, he was moving inside her in long strong pumps of his penis. She was exhausted. She should be beyond arousal, but somehow she wasn't. Each stroke was an electric shock.

"I love being inside you, darlin'," John whispered in his dark, black magic voice. "It's like you were made just for me. I can't keep my hands off you." She could feel his lips moving against her skin, the puffs of air as he spoke. The smell of sex rose, sharp and pungent, in the air. Normally fastidious, she should have been appalled, but now all she could do was open wider for him, clutch his shoulders for balance as the speed and depth of his strokes increased.

It started as a flutter, ballooning into warmth, then exploded in a fireball of heat. All of a sudden, she couldn't breathe, couldn't move. This couldn't be happening again, not so soon, not so quickly. She'd never...

Suzanne stilled and cried out, throbbing with intense, almost painful pleasure. It went on and on. John's steady movements kept her on the edge for so long she thought she would faint from the pleasure-pain. After what felt like hours, he licked the skin behind her ear, lightly bit the lobe, then whispered, "It's got to be hard and fast now, darlin'. I can't control myself much longer. But if I get on top, I'll pound you through the mattress. Gotta be from behind."

She could barely understand his words. What was he talking about? That—that unbridled lovemaking, hot and hard—that had been controlling himself?

When he pulled out of her, she felt a sudden emptiness. But there was no time to mourn the loss of his body in hers. He flipped her over, stuffed both pillows under her stomach and lifted her hips. Her muscles were lax, rubbery. She couldn't react, could barely move. He moved her like a little doll.

His knees slid between hers, opening them and then suddenly he was there, slamming in so hard and fast she gasped.

He gave a few experimental thrusts. He slid in deep and stopped, touching her womb. He rotated his hips, measuring her sheath, testing her for wetness and reception.

"Not yet," he muttered. Bending forward, he wrapped one strong arm around her. "You need to come one more time."

His hand moved through the folds of her sex, touching her where she was clenched around his penis, then sliding up where he caressed—so, so carefully—her clitoris. It was like being struck by lightning. Suzanne stiffened and moaned.

"Oh, yeah," he breathed. Though the pad of his finger was rough, his touch was delicate, as were the light rocking motions he made inside her. Slipping in and out, barely moving, in time with his sliding thumb on her clitoris...

She stopped breathing, stopped thinking, stopped seeing…everything inside her clenched, gathered…

And leapt. Her heart started pounding as she pulsed around him. A hard, tense orgasm, which brought tears to her eyes. Her cry was muffled against the mattress. He held himself still, tightly wedged inside her, unmoving until she quieted. She lay with her forehead against the mattress, trying to catch her breath.

Finally, Suzanne arched her neck to look behind her—and froze.

"Brace yourself, because I'm going to do you hard. Grab the bedstead." His deep voice was choked, almost unrecognizable. The softly liquid southern intonations were gone.

He looked frighteningly dangerous. His features were sharp with arousal. Red flags rode his cheekbones and his lips were dark with blood. His eyes—glittering shards—watched her with laser-sharp intensity. The huge muscles in his shoulders and biceps were corded with tension as he held her hips with his hands, clutching so tightly she knew she'd be bruised later.

Even if she wanted to, there was no turning back, no escaping his powerful grip. She searched his face for traces of mercy and found none. No softness, no sign of affection. Just pure lust. A strong, rampant male in full rut. Whatever was going to happen next was completely out of her control.

And maybe out of his.

She felt so vulnerable, so completely open, crouching there with her backside in the air. They touched in only three places. His knees keeping hers wide apart, his hands clenched on her hips and his penis in her sheath.

His knees pushed hers further apart, and he tightened his grip on her hips. She could feel the dark crisp hairs of his thighs against the inside of hers, the hair around his sex against her bottom. In this position she couldn't control the depth or rhythm of his thrusts. She was totally and completely at his mercy.

It seemed as if the whole world were still. Silent. Dark. Waiting for a sign.

Suzanne studied his face, the strength and the lust and the frightening male blankness. It was too much for her. She closed her eyes, turned and buried her head in the mattress. Her hands reached up, fingers curling around the bars of the bedstead.

It was a signal—of submission, of surrender. He bucked, once, and she grunted. For a moment, she thought he would stop, but then he moved, suddenly and furiously, pumping hard and fast.

Afterwards, she never knew how long it lasted. An hour, two hours, all night. There was no way of telling. He rammed into her mercilessly, endlessly, using the full strength of his body. On and on in a steady, driving rhythm. The bed creaked so much with the force of his thrusts she was vaguely surprised it didn't collapse.

No limits. And there seemed to be no limits to the pleasure he was able to call forth from her. She climaxed over and over again, completely out of control of her own body.

Just when she thought she couldn't take any more, when her trembling and sweaty hands were losing their grip on the iron rods of the bedstead, when her throat burned from the gasps and her nipples were rubbed raw from the sheet, she felt him swell, grow even harder. With a shout, he erupted inside her. His rough hands clamped around her hips were the only things holding her up. He ground hard against her as he came and groaned as if he were dying.

She felt like she was dying herself, completely outside herself, completely beyond the bounds of what she'd always considered herself.

"Jesus." The word was half-whisper, half-moan as John collapsed on top of her, his heavy weight pinning her to the mattress. He was sweaty and smelled of musk. His penis, even now partially erect, still lay in her and she could feel the wetness of his semen trickling out of her vagina, along her thighs.

She felt his large hand brushing over her tangled hair, the tickle of his breath over her bare shoulder as he sighed and then nothing more as sleep claimed her.

Chapter Eleven

It was barely dawn when John awoke. He was a soldier and was used to waking up instantly alert. They used to practice it—he'd keep his men sleep—deprived for days, then test marksmanship a few minutes after waking them up, minutes into REM sleep. John himself didn't have problems. He was good at that, good at being able to focus instantly on the new day.

Now, though his mind was alert, his body foolishly wanted to simply stay in bed, curled around Suzanne's back.

She didn't move when she slept. He couldn't hear her breathing but he could feel it, one hand curled around her rib cage, fingers just brushing the soft underside of her breast. She was impossibly soft and delicate, almost too much so, for the use he'd made of her through the night. His cock stirred at the memory and he pulled her even closer, burying his face against the delicate skin of her neck. His beard rasped against that pale, fragile skin and he pulled back. He didn't want to give her whisker burn.

He lay still, savoring the moment. That, too, was a soldier's trick. In the field, any moment could be your last. Your senses opened, each sight, sound, taste, smell razor-sharp and intense.

This wasn't a firebase, but danger still threatened. Which is why, though he'd rather just lie here forever, curled around Suzanne, he had to get up. Contact Bud to see if there had been any developments. Check the perimeter. Get his men in on the investigation.

Pete and Les wouldn't be as hampered as Bud in getting info. Bud had to obey the law. Pete and Les had to obey him and he was a hell of a lot more demanding than the law. Particularly when it came to protecting Suzanne Barron.

Detaching himself from Suzanne proved harder than he thought. His hands simply didn't want to leave her. He usually rolled out of bed two seconds after waking up, but now he simply lay there, stroking her skin, smelling her hair, feeling her warmth.

Finally, when the sky started turning pink outside the window, he forced himself out of the bed. Padding naked into the bathroom, he wet a washcloth with warm water and walked back to the bed. He stood for a moment, looking down.

There were smudges under her eyes, half-hidden by the long, lush eyelashes and a few bruises on her hips he'd given her towards the end. At some level, he knew he shouldn't have used her as much and as hard as he had. He couldn't regret it, however. If someone had put an AK-47 to his head last night, he would have been totally incapable of stopping.

He bent down and rolled her carefully onto her back. She was so exhausted she didn't wake up.

He gently cleaned her between the legs. He'd come three times in her and she was sticky. He wiped her carefully, trying hard not to wake her up.

This is something he should have done last night, but he'd been too wiped out to do anything but collapse on top of her and fall into a sleep so deep it felt like a coma.

She was so beautiful, even here. The folds of her sex were soft, the palest pink, surrounded by ash-brown pubic hairs interspersed with gold. His breathing sped up as he imagined kissing her there, licking her, sucking the little clitoris he could see when he opened her a up a bit with two fingers.

Such mysterious folds of flesh, so simple and yet the source of such mind-blowing delight. He wanted to sink to his knees and bury his face between her thighs. He wanted to lick her until she shook with the force of her orgasm, as she'd done last night.

God, it had been so exciting to feel her pulling on his cock with her cunt while she came, shuddering…

He had a hard-on. Again. If he followed his instincts, he'd slip back into bed with her, mount her, pull her legs apart and start moving the instant he entered her. With any other woman, he would have. He'd never, ever pulled his punches with women. They knew right upfront what to expect.

He made sure the women he had realized he had a strong sex drive and that they were going to be used hard. If that's what they wanted, fine. If not, there were plenty of other women around.

They knew what they were in for and he hadn't had many complaints. So if this hadn't been Suzanne, he'd be in her right now, watching her wake up to the feel of his cock moving in her.

But this was Suzanne. He wasn't too sure what made her different from the others, but there it was—she was different.

She was tired, and needed her sleep, and that took absolute precedence over his iron-hard cock. He pulled the covers up over her, watched her for another moment, easing a pale curl away from her eyes with a movement, which became a caress, then forced himself away.

A quick shower, shave and cup of coffee later, and he was in his underground lair.

Bud wasn't going to dance with joy at being woken up this early, but tough shit.

"Morrison." Bud's voice was annoyed but alert.

"John here. What have you got for me?" The long silence had John sitting up straight. "What?"

"You're not going to like it, Midnight."

"There are a lot of things I don't like about the situation. So spill."

"Suzanne worked off and on with another decorator, a guy called Todd Armstrong. And before you go off the deep end, he was gay. Nice guy, though. Smart. I met him a few times. He was fun."

There was a bad feeling in the pit of John's stomach. "Was?"

Bud sighed. "Yeah. Guy was wasted. Portland PD found his body about six hours ago. He'd been tortured, Midnight. It wasn't pretty."

Every signal John's body could send was in overdrive. The hairs on his forearms were standing straight up. Bud was right. This was bad.

Bud's lover, Suzanne's girlfriend—what was her name?...Claire. That was it. "You'd better watch out for Claire, then," John said. "It looks like everyone around Suzanne is getting wasted."

"Done. I've got people watching Claire 24/7 and she's not a happy camper."

"Tough." Like Bud, John had no trouble at all prioritizing. Bud's girlfriend might not be thrilled at the prospect of being restricted in her movements, but her safety came first. Second and third, too. Bud knew that and had taken steps to make sure she'd live. Anything else was bullshit. "What about Suzanne's parents?"

"I'm on it. They live in Baja California. I've contacted the Mexican police and they've posted discreet guards."

"Okay." John grappled with the size of the threat against Suzanne. If Bud had called in the Mexican police, he was scared. "What have we got to go on here?"

"Damn all." Bud's voice was ripe with frustration. "Everything's a dead end. We've got the name of both shooters, but there must have been a cutout, because there's no paper trail. No unusual payments in their bank account, no unusual prints in their apartment, no phone records, nothing. Nada. Zip."

"The money's in the Caymans. Or in Liechtenstein," John said. "And long gone. You're playing with your own dick."

"Yeah, well if I am, I'm not having any fun. Goddamn it, we need to know what's going on. Pump Suzanne, Midnight. Find out what it is that she knows, or what it is that she's got, which is dangerous enough to kill for. And do it fast. Claire's involved and I'm not having her exposed to danger. So find out what she knows, or I'll have your ass in a sling."

John could hear the ripe fear for Claire behind Bud's hard words, otherwise he would have handed Bud his head on a stick. It wasn't something he'd have understood a week ago, but now he did. Anything that threatened his woman was guaranteed to drive him crazy.

"Okay. I'll be in touch." John thumbed the off button on his cell and sat back, thinking.

This was a mission. He could do missions—he'd done them all his life. So why was this creating a problem for him?

Because it was Suzanne.

Because he couldn't think straight around her. It wasn't just a question of thinking with his cock, though of course there was that. He couldn't keep his hands off the woman but it was more than that.

Fear for her skewed his thinking processes, threw him completely off-kilter. Worse, off-mission. How could he think straight when the thought of anything happening to her had his heart pounding and provoked that swooping feeling of a mortar round exploding ten feet away?

He called Pete and pulled his men off all current cases. From this moment on, his team had to be as concentrated as a laser on Suzanne Barron. By nightfall, John knew they'd have everything that could be known about her, including her high school grades, spending patterns and menstrual cycle.

Today he needed to grill her. He'd avoided it, putting it off, distracted by the sex. He couldn't afford that now, he thought as he headed upstairs.

But first, he needed to feed her. She hadn't eaten in 24 hours. Though he was a lousy cook, he did keep some supplies on hand. Coffee, eggs, vacuum-packed bacon, bread. Once she'd eaten, they'd talk.

As always, it felt good to have a plan, even a half-assed one. He had bread in the toaster, eggs in a bowl and the coffee maker on when he placed the bacon in the pan. It spat, little pinpricks of fire on his chest and arms.

"Son of a bitch!" He scrambled for something to cover the pan with.

"That's why women wear aprons," a soft, amused voice said from behind him. "I wouldn't advise cooking bacon bare-chested."

He spun around, ignoring the flying grease. She was standing in the doorway. In a blue nightgown this time, a twin to the one he'd ripped. She'd showered. He could smell her across the room, over the bacon and the toast... the charred toast—shit! He burned his fingers digging the slices out of the toaster.

All the while he watched her carefully. He'd used her pretty hard last night. He hadn't been able to control himself at the end. He had no idea what her reaction this morning would be.

But she was smiling at him, crossing the room bare-footed, brushing by him and making every hormone in his body stand up and clamor for more of what he'd had all night.

"I guess that's not a gun and that you're really glad to see me."

He didn't have to guess at what she meant. His cock did what it usually did when it saw her. Or smelled her. Or thought of her. He swelled as he watched her.

She reached across and turned down the heat. The bacon stopped spitting and settled down to cooking. She turned, humming softly, to his cabinets.

Some feminine magic led her unerringly to where he kept the plates. It was amazing. She'd never been here before and yet she moved around the little kitchenette as if she lived here. A few minutes later the table was set.

Actually set. As properly as his equipment would allow.

He usually ate over the sink. But she tore off paper towels to make mats, put the silverware on either side of the plates and placed two mugs carefully on the right hand side of each plate. She even put platters out for the bacon and the toast and the eggs. Amazing.

Sex wasn't going to happen right now. That was okay, because they needed to talk, but his cock wasn't too convinced. Under the table, it stayed hard and aching. He ignored it because he had to.

He poured her coffee while she filled his plate. He was starved. She must have been, too, though she managed to eat daintily.

His teeth crunched on something. "Some egg shell got into the scrambled eggs," he mumbled. "Sorry."

"Yes," she said serenely, forking another clump of eggs onto his plate and then hers. "And you oversalted the eggs and burned the toast. But you're forgiven. Have we exhausted the food supplies?"

"Pretty much. We'll have to make a food run into Fork in the Road some time today."

She considered him, head to one side, silver eyes observing him soberly, and then nodded. "Okay. I need to buy some stuff anyway."

Female stuff, he'd bet. She could buy whatever she wanted as long as he didn't have to know about it. If it was female stuff, he didn't want to go there.

Suzanne pushed her plate to one side and leaned forward, searching his eyes. "So. Tell me the truth, John. I need to know. For my peace of mind, if nothing else. How long are we going to have to stay here?"

"As long as it takes," he answered bluntly. He debated, briefly, telling her about Todd Armstrong, then decided against it. She had a right to know, and she'd be angry later. But now it was his call and he decided not to overwhelm her. He needed her to think straight and she wasn't going to do that knowing a friend was dead, because of her. "We're going to have to figure out what's going on, honey. As long as we're in the dark, we're vulnerable. I need to ask you some questions."

She nodded, poured herself another cup of coffee and folded her hands on the table. "Go ahead and ask." She looked at him and waited.

John didn't try to soften his words or pussyfoot around it. "Two men were sent to kill you. Do you have any idea why?"

She was still a long moment, and then shook her head. "No. Absolutely not. I've thought and thought and thought, but I can't imagine why anyone would want to hurt me."

"Okay. Let's take it step by step. Let's start with your job. What is it exactly that you do?"

She sighed. "I guess the easiest way to describe what I do is that I design spaces, both public and private. Not everyone has the time or inclination to decorate their office or home, so they call in a specialist. Me. I'll visit the space to be decorated, come up with two or three alternatives and the client chooses which alternative he or she wants. Sometimes it's an individual and sometimes it's a committee. Then I arrange for the purchase of the furniture and with the help of a moving company, I'm there to set everything up."

"Who are your clients?"

"Mainly people in the business community. Some private clients. I've helped in the design of three shops—two boutiques and a bookstore—and a couple of museums, too. It's really tame stuff."

John walked her through her clients over the past year, grilling her on every aspect of her job. She'd never worked for government agencies or for public procurement companies or defense manufacturers. Not even a software company. She wasn't privy to any industrial secrets. She earned well but not spectacularly well. She had a small nest egg in the bank, but nothing that was worth killing for. John earned more than that per job. She'd built her business slowly, through word of mouth. Her clients were all solid citizens.

An hour later, frustrated, John rubbed the back of his neck. If there was any person on the face of the earth who had an innocuous job and a perfectly harmless life, looks like it was Suzanne.

Now for the biggie, the one he hated. He had to ask it and was dreading the answer.

"How about your love life? Any disgruntled ex-lovers, abusive former boyfriends?" John asked the question casually, but his fists were clenched under the table.

"Oh." Suzanne looked surprised at the idea. "No, of course not." She blushed, delightfully, but kept her eyes on his. "I, um—" She stopped and drew in a big breath. "I haven't…dated all that much. My mom was sick while I was in college and we were all pretty much caught up in her illness. Luckily, she's fine now. And the past few years I've been concentrated on work."

"Who's the last guy you were seeing?"

"John…is this necessary?"

"Absolutely." That was a lie. John didn't know how necessary this was to the investigation. But it was certainly necessary to his peace of mind to have names to put to faces. The thought of another man's hands on her made him sick with rage. As soon as he got a name or two he'd check them out and make damn sure they never approached Suzanne ever again.

"Okay. I guess the last man I dated was Marcus Freeman. He's my bank manager. But it's not—well, it was a very casual relationship. We never, um…we never—you know:" She shrugged. "The last man I, um, had a sexual relationship was Adrian Whitby, the director of the Kronen Museum. I designed their new annex. That was two years ago. We broke it off and I haven't seen him since."

Les was going to have to check Adrian Whitby out. John would be too tempted to smash his face in. He could maybe stomach checking Marcus Freeman out, knowing he and

Suzanne hadn't gone to bed together. The thought of another man kissing Suzanne, the thought that this creep Whitby's cock had been in her, enraged him.

Suzanne was his. No other man was ever going to get within two feet of her. John realized he'd kill to keep it that way.

He sipped his coffee, needing to get his emotions under control, get his voice calm. Rage wasn't a productive emotion. He sipped again and forced himself to concentrate.

"What about your family? Does your father do any sensitive work? Your brother? Sister?"

Suzanne shook her head. "We're a small family. I'm an only child. My father is a retired college professor of literature, an expert in Chaucer. My mother is—was—a high school French teacher. She's half French herself. They retired to Baja California, where Dad is writing what he fondly considers will be the Great American Novel. They're perfectly pleasant, utterly harmless people."

Another dead end. Shit. This wasn't getting them anywhere. Frustration was an unusual emotion for him and he didn't like it one bit. John pinched the bridge of his nose.

She'd answered his questions calmly, but he could tell she was upset. He didn't want her upset.

What the hell?

How was it that all of a sudden Suzanne's serenity was more important to him than information? This had never happened before. He'd never ever had any difficulty in keeping emotion separate from a mission. But there it was—he couldn't stand to see her unhappy.

There was no precedent for these feelings in his life. What was going on? He needed to pump her, to push her harder and…he couldn't.

There she was, at his table. Heartbreakingly beautiful and forlorn. A unicorn at the edge of the forest. He didn't want her worried and he didn't want her sad.

He'd walked knowingly into danger more times than he could count. He'd faced hostile gunfire. He'd even once defused a bomb. There wasn't anything he'd back down from, anything he feared—or so he'd thought. And yet seeing Suzanne sitting in his kitchen chair, looking forlorn and frightened was more than he could bear.

He'd have sworn he didn't have a heart, but there it was, clenching tightly in his chest.

Moving fast, he scooped Suzanne up in his arms and placed her on his lap. After an initial cry of surprise, Suzanne slumped in his arms, and put her head on his shoulder. They sat there in the calm quiet morning light. Just the feel of her in his arms, listening to her quiet breathing, pressing her head against his shoulder, calmed down something sore and inflamed deep down inside of him.

He ran the back of his forefinger down the sleeve of her nightgown, and then fingered it. It was an excuse to keep his hands on her. "That's a pretty color. You look great in blue." It was true. But then any color would look good on her.

"Thank you." She turned her face up to him and smiled. "But it's not blue."

John looked at the pinch of material in his hand. It was blue. He raised his eyes to hers. She shook her head. Okay. Not blue. He looked back down. Yes, it was. Dammit, it was blue.

She covered his hand with hers. She was smiling up at him, looking for a moment like the woman he'd first met. Confident. Sexy. He loved seeing her like this. He'd give his right arm to keep that expression on her face.

"You have problems with colors, John. You need to learn the names, the nuances. For example, this nightgown isn't blue, it's robin's egg. There are so many blues around: powder, peacock, navy, denim, Wedgwood..."

He was trying not to smile. "Okay, okay, I get it."

"The world has a thousand colors." She ran her hand over his bare chest, down his arm. "Let's take your skin. You're very tanned. I'd say your skin color is…" she cocked her head. "Earth. Maybe bark where you get more exposure to the sun. But here…" She traced a finger along his biceps, and then around to the paler skin beneath, "here I'd say you're more a suede. I can see all sorts of different colors in you, from your hair, which is definitely ebony, with traces of pewter along the temples, to your eyes, which are gunmetal. Mouth." Shifting in his arms, finger over his lips. The smile had changed and was no longer amused, it was pure temptation. That was the smile that got Adam into so much trouble with the snake. Her voice dropped to a whisper. "Your mouth is…oh, I'd say cinnamon." Her finger caressed the outlines of his lips. Her finger dipped into his mouth and he sucked the tip. His tongue swirled around it, exactly as it did to her nipple and he knew that's what she was remembering by the way her lids lowered over her silvery gray eyes.

She had pure devil in her expression and he—there was no way to hide it any more—he was excited as hell. She looked down at his lap and—what a witch she was—licked her lips. His hard-on lengthened. It occurred to him that she was going to use sex as a way to forget her troubles.

Great. Worked for him.

There wasn't anything that needed doing that couldn't be put off for an hour. Or two. Or four. He could get into sex, big time.

Both her hands were in his hair now, fingers curled around his head. She ran her tongue around his lips and he obediently, eagerly opened his mouth. Her tongue rubbed against his.

"Mmm," she whispered, angling her head, kissing him deeply.

Oh, yeah.

She pulled away just as he moved to pull her closer.

"Ah, ah," she admonished, lips so close to his he could feel her warm breath, running her hands down his arms to pin his hands to his side, "no touching during the color lesson." She exerted a little pressure on his wrists, as if to say—stay put.

He let her pin him down. It was ridiculous of course. There was no way she could force him to keep his hands off her, no way she could match his strength, but if this gave her a measure of control, when her life was spiraling out of control, then what the hell.

So he sat with Suzanne on his lap, his cock in its usual condition whenever this woman touched him, or was close to him, or even looked at him—iron hard.

The minx knew it, of course. How could she not know it, when she was sitting right over his hard-on? But she ignored it, as she continued playing with his mouth, petting him all over.

She ran her tongue around the rim of his ear, the tip following the whorls to the center, while her hands caressed his shoulders. It electrified him to feel her small wet tongue delicately probing. The hairs on the nape of his neck rose.

"Let's see here," she sighed. She found his right nipple in the chest hair and rubbed it. Damn, it was like an electric jolt shooting straight to his cock. She breathed in deeply, her breasts rubbing against him, as she fingered his nipple. "I'd say, here..." A pink-tipped finger rubbing around the flat aureole, "here you're brick, with copper tones, but here—" her head dipped and she licked him, and then suckled gently, "Mm. Vermilion. Definitely."

It wasn't just his cock that was hard. He was hard all over, tense and tight. Clenched like a fist. Each slow, lazy lick, each pull of her mouth on his nipple shot straight to his groin.

With a smile and a sigh, she slipped off his lap, kneeling at his feet. Reaching up to his pectorals, she ran her hands over his chest, over his abdomen. The witch bit lightly at the muscles of his abdomen.

"Bay, bronze," she whispered and her little pink tongue ran over his chest and belly to his belly button. "Sand." The tip of her tongue fit into his belly button and she bit him, again, not so lightly this time. Her chin rubbed against his cock.

Oh God.

A pull of the strings, and the waistband of his sweats opened. She pulled the sweats down and took him in hand.

"The prize," she breathed and pulled his cock away from his belly. She ran her fisted hand down it, then back up. Slowly. Again. And again.

He was dying.

Her eyes narrowed as she studied him. "All sorts of colors," she murmured. "A rainbow of them. Tea, fudge, cognac." She cupped his balls then ran her finger up his cock to the tip. He was wet, a second from coming.

Slowly, as if she had all the time in the world, Suzanne circled the tip, around and around…"And here…" her voice was a seductive whisper as she looked up at him, eyes flashing pure silver, "plum."

She bent, took him in her mouth and sucked.

John exploded out of his chair, pulling her up and carrying her, with every intention of going to the bedroom. He didn't make it.

He only got as far as the kitchen wall, where he shoved his sweatpants down, pulled her nightgown up and plunged into her. She was wet and soft, as if she'd come. Maybe she had, while she'd been sucking his cock. It didn't make any difference because he had no self-control at all. He didn't even try to moderate his strokes, just pounded into her. It was so hard and fast and furious it couldn't last long. She moaned, and then cried. When her cunt began gripping him in long liquid pulls, he slammed into her one last time and held himself deep inside her, grinding into her as he came.

They stood there, their breathing loud in the room. John hitched her legs higher around his waist, waiting for some strength to return to his legs and some blood to return to his head.

Her hair shifted on his shoulder as she turned her head into his neck, biting him lightly and sighing.

She kissed his shoulder and whispered, "You know, John, maybe you should see someone about this wall fetish you have."

Chapter Twelve

"John, I want a tree."

It was dusk and John was putting the shopping away, his kitchen organization appalling. He kept flour next to washing detergent and sugar next to Ajax, but Suzanne held her tongue.

They'd taken a run down to Fork in the Road, which had proved just as cosmopolitan as its name would suggest. A gas station with annexed diner, four houses, a post office and—oddly enough—a well-equipped little supermarket, probably the only one in a hundred square miles. She'd found everything she needed, and now she had to send John out. There were things she wanted to do and he'd just be in the way. Besides, she wanted to surprise him a little.

The trip to Fork in the Road had been quite an experience.

He'd morphed immediately into Midnight Man the instant they'd set foot outside the shack. The man who'd groaned and shook as he made love to her disappeared, as if he had never existed. The man who took his place was as cold and controlled as a cyborg. Each movement measured, economical, physical grace in action. He had a knack of being aware of everything that was going on. 'Situation awareness' she'd once heard it called and it applied to fighter pilots. To SEALs, too, it appeared.

He'd been silent on the drive down, concentrated on the driving, constantly checking the rear view mirrors. In the small town, he'd gone into an elaborate ballet every time they moved. It had taken her an hour to realize that he was making sure she was never exposed to gunfire. That, in any attempt on her life, the bullet would go through him first.

It had brought tears to her eyes, which she'd instantly tried to hide. But the Midnight Man was nothing if not observant, damn him. He'd immediately asked what was wrong and she'd had to make some nonsense up about catching a cold. After which, notwithstanding her protestations, she'd had to walk around all afternoon with his heavy sheepskin jacket around her shoulders, covering her hands and falling to her knees.

She'd taken her time at the store, filling five shopping bags full of the things she wanted. He'd looked curiously at the bags, then reached for his wallet.

"Oh no," Suzanne had protested. This was stuff she wanted to buy, after all. "Let me—"

He'd shot her a look so appalled at the idea that she should pay, she'd burst out with laughter in the supermarket, a bored checkout clerk looking on.

So they'd done their shopping, had a late afternoon sandwich and coffee at the diner—with John sitting with his back to the wall, coldly observing everyone who came into the place—and driven back without incident as light drained from the sky.

Now her bags were waiting in the small kitchen and she needed him to go out for a while. She also needed a tree.

John stopped his movements and looked at her. "You want a what?"

"Tree, John. It's Christmas Eve. We need a tree."

He looked so dumbfounded; it was as if he'd never heard the words 'Christmas' and 'tree' together.

She sighed. "Look, it's Christmas Eve. We're tired and stressed and need a little lightness and joy in our lives. I've never spent a Christmas Eve in my life without a tree, and I have no intention of starting now. Whatever is going on, I've been deprived of my home and my job, and so have you. But I won't be deprived of Christmas. Or a Christmas tree. I really need one. Don't you celebrate Christmas?"

He just stared at her as if he couldn't understand the words. And maybe he couldn't. Sad as it sounded, maybe there hadn't been that many Christmas trees in his life.

It was a remarkable insight into his character. He seemed so strong and self-sufficient, so beyond the ordinary human being's fears and desires. So tough, so controlled. Suzanne suspected there hadn't been much softness in his life. "Where were you last Christmas?" she asked, gently.

He shrugged indifferently. "OUTCONUS. That's Outside the Continental US. In Afghanistan, actually. It's a remarkably treeless country. Christmas is just another day in the military."

Something tugged at her heart, hard. John was a man who hadn't allowed himself much in life. He'd had a hard life of duty and sacrifice. He needed a Christmas celebration perhaps more than she did.

"Well, this place certainly isn't treeless," Suzanne said, with a nod outside the cabin window, where stands of trees stood thick and green in the waning light. "So I'd like you to please dig one up for me—not chop it down. Dig around the roots and put them in a burlap bag if you have one."

"I don't want to leave you," he growled.

She laid a hand on his powerful forearm. It was like touching pure coiled energy. The feel of him beneath her hand excited her so much she almost forgot what she was saying. She looked up into his eyes. "I'll stay right here," she said. "And you could get me one of those trees growing right near to the house. You can keep an eye on the cabin all the time."

She could not only see him struggle with the idea of leaving her alone, she could feel it in his muscles. His forearm felt like tensed steel under her hand. Maybe it was the intense sex, maybe it was the intense situation, which had thrown them together under pressure, but she felt she knew him so well she could almost read his mind. He didn't want to do this, didn't want to leave her alone for a minute—it suddenly occurred to her that he hadn't left her, not even for a second, since the night of the intruder—but also realized it was a perfectly reasonable request.

His jaw, bristly now at the end of the day, worked as he struggled with the desire to please her, which required leaving her alone and defenseless. Two mutually incompatible concepts.

She shouldn't be putting him through this strain, but she needed the relief of a Christmas celebration and perhaps so did he.

"Please," she whispered.

She needed so desperately to create a little oasis of peace and pleasure, to feel something other than hunted prey. Even if only for a few hours. It was Christmas, her favorite time of year. She'd celebrated Christmas all her life. It was a big event in the Barron family. If she couldn't celebrate Christmas, her unknown and unseen enemy had already won. He'd stripped her of her humanity and turned her into a cowering animal. She gently squeezed his arm.

"Please," she said again, watching him. There was nothing else to say. She didn't wheedle or try to explain why it was so important to her. Either he understood or didn't. She knew instinctively that John couldn't be forced to do something he didn't want to. Giving in to her entirely reasonable request was something he had to want to do all on his own.

His muscles bunched and quivered. His jaw clenched hard. She could feel his reluctance in his muscles, see it on his face. She smiled up at him, and then stretched to kiss the corner of his mouth. It was like kissing a wooden statue. She kissed him again. "Come on. You know you don't have to be out of sight of the cabin. I'll be perfectly safe. You told me I was safe here, right?"

"Yeah." It was as if the word had been wrenched out of his chest with huge red-hot pincers.

"Well, then. You see? What can happen?"

His mouth opened to argue and she decided to whip out the big guns. Pulling his head down, she stood on tiptoe and kissed him. Open-mouthed, her tongue deep in his mouth, full body frontal. He wasn't wooden any more; he was male heat and sinew, darkness and power and desire. She ate at his mouth, moving hotly against him as he swelled erect.

He was so amazingly large. She rubbed her belly against him, feeling him lengthen even further and was surprised that she'd been able to take him. The memory of his heavy penis inside her, thrusting hard, melted her bones. A hot liquid pull of her vaginal muscles made her shudder.

She was tempted. Very tempted. But there were things to do.

She pulled her mouth away, a fraction of an inch. Just enough so she could form the word, but close enough for him to feel her breath. "Tree."

He looked down at her, face strained. His lips were suffused with blood and wet from her mouth. One big hand on her backside pulled her towards him as he ground against her. She fluttered inside, and looked helplessly up at him. "John." There wasn't any air in her lungs. The word came out more as a stirring of the air than a sound.

He arched his head away from her, neck tendons corded, jaws clenching. He looked at the ceiling for a long moment, and brought his head back down as he stepped back reluctantly, frowning. "You're going to use sex to get everything you want from me, aren't you?"

She didn't even have to think about it. "Yes."

"It works, damn it," he grumbled. He reached for his sheepskin jacket and stopped, pointing a finger at her. "I don't want you going anywhere," he growled.

"Of course not." She smiled innocently. "Where would I go, anyway? Look, I'm staying right here, you will be in sight of the cabin at all times, nothing will happen except that we get ourselves a Christmas tree and feel better."

He stared at her, as if she were going to pull a rabbit out of a hat. Or run away into the forest. He gave a sudden nod, pulled on thick leather gloves and walked out the door.

She needed this, but she knew what it cost him. He had an overly protective nature. This went completely against the grain of every instinct he had. It was a promising sign that he'd gone out to look for a tree for her. It showed that there was room for compromise in his hard nature.

Suzanne sprang into action. She didn't have much time. It would take her hours to dig up a tree with the roots, place it in a bag and haul it into the cabin. But John was stronger than most and was frighteningly efficient. So she had to hurry.

In half an hour, a turkey leg was basting in the oven together with baked potatoes. Frozen biscuits were waiting to be put in, corn on the cob was boiling on the stove and an apple pie was waiting to be baked. It was frozen, but a good brand. Vanilla ice cream was in the small freezer.

A bowl of unbuttered popcorn awaited threading. Apples studded with cloves were in a bowl, adding their spice to the air.

The Fork in the Road supermarket had even had a surprisingly decent selection of wines. One bottle was boiling gently on the stove, steeped in sugar, cloves and cinnamon. She breathed in the heady air of vin brulè and smiled. The other bottle was airing.

It wasn't Comme Chez Soi, but it would do. Now the shack.

This place was so bleak, so spare. So unloving and unloved, it hurt her heart.

Opening the bags, she spread out the supplies. Three cheap single-bed red sheets billowed out. She tied them with decorative knots over the sorry, dull brown sofa and two armchairs, placed red and white striped pillows on them and arranged them together in the middle of the room, creating a pleasing little grouping. John had simply shoved them against the walls. An upended wooden crate she'd found outside the kitchen door covered with two pretty oversized linen tea towels made a makeshift coffee table.

She'd found a lovely rose-patterned tablecloth and napkins with big cabbage roses on them for the dining table. Two taper candles in cut-glass holders and the table looked almost…elegant.

She'd made John stop by the roadside on the way back. As he watched, astounded, she'd used a knife he kept in the SUV to cut boughs of evergreens. She put the boughs in a big plastic vase filled with water, and put it beside the sofa. The fresh smell of pine soon permeated the living room. She lit two big red perfumed candles and placed them on the coffee table and lit a line of votive candles she'd arranged on a shelf. She twirled the knobs of the radio until she found a station playing Christmas music.

Hurry! Everything had to be just so by the time John returned, including herself. A quick shower and application of perfumed body lotion. Check. Cherry-red cashmere sweater. Check. Lightly-applied makeup - the first she'd worn in two days. Check. Perfume on her pulse points, hair, between her breasts. Check. She had just finished brushing her hair when she heard the front door open and hurried into the living room.

It had turned dark and very cold while she'd made her preparations. John stood in the doorframe, a good-sized tree with its roots attached over one shoulder, a large tin tub hanging from one big hand, looking for all the world like Paul Bunyan minus the ox. A gust of frigid, pine-scented air gusted in behind him. His breath swirled whitely around his head.

He took in the room and her in one dark glance and something—something dark and powerful—moved in his eyes. He froze in place, face hard and set as he looked at her.

Oh God.

She'd wanted so much to surprise him, delight him. Make him forget his woes, and hers. Clearly, she'd overstepped the bounds. With a quick rush of shame, Suzanne realized that trying to 'fix up' his shack was an implicit criticism of it. As if she were too refined to spend time in a place that was less than designer perfect. He must think she was a terrible snob. Snobbery was the farthest thing from her mind. It was so instinctive for her—to make her surroundings better, to prettify—that it hadn't even occurred to her that he might take it badly.

The last thing she wanted to do was offend him. He'd risked his life for her. He'd abandoned his business without a backward glance in order to protect her. He'd taught her more about sex and passion in the past few days than she'd learned in 28 years of life. The thought that she'd insulted this magnificent man made her heart-stricken.

They stared at each other across the room.

"I'm sorry, John," she whispered. "Did I overstep the bounds? I thought I'd surprise you." She was wringing her hands and forced herself to stop. "I hope I didn't offend you if I changed a few things around. I didn't want to insult you, I just -"

"No." His voice was hoarse. He cleared his throat and moved into the room. "No, I'm not offended. Of course not. Everything's very…nice. Where do you want this?"

"Over there." Suzanne pointed to the corner that positively cried out for a Christmas tree. "Put some water in the tub first."

"Yes, ma'am." He actually smiled, perhaps the third smile she'd seen cross his face. Her heart turned over. And just like that she knew. She was in love with this man.

She must have been half-way there already because the knowledge settled in her heart not as a blinding revelation, but as if there were a John Huntington-shaped place already there, waiting for him to fill it and waiting for her to acknowledge it.

Was this why she hadn't given her heart to any other man? Because she hadn't, not really. Oh sure, she'd dated and had had a few lovers, but right now, at this moment, she couldn't remember a thing about any of them. She remembered everything—everything—about John Huntington.

The way his deep voice seemed to set up reverberations in her diaphragm. The way his hard, callused hands could be so delicate. The way he unerringly put himself between her and danger. The way his tongue against hers robbed her of breath. The way his penis felt, hard and hot, inside her.

Was it just sex? Maybe. Goodness knows, she'd thought of sex the instant she'd seen him. They hadn't had one conversation that hadn't had sex as the backdrop. It oozed out of the man's pores and she'd fallen instantly in lust, the second she'd met him. So unlike her, the Queen of Cool.

Whenever she'd thought about finding the love of her life, she'd imagined some nice, suitable man, whose tastes were similar to hers. They'd date for a month or two, going to recently reviewed restaurants and first-run movies. They'd go to bed together, discreetly, tastefully, and find they liked the same brand of coffee and plain croissants for breakfast. They'd read the same books and vote the same party.

Nothing could be further from that scenario than John. He wasn't a nice, suitable man. He was a warrior, a hard, tough man. They probably didn't read the same books and didn't have the same taste in music. And they very definitely didn't vote for the same party.

Instead of dating for a few months, they'd had wild sex the day they'd met. In bed, he was overwhelming, a force of nature, not the gentle and tame lover of her imagination. Nothing about him was easy or comfortable or familiar.

And yet she loved him. She felt more for him, a man she'd known for a few days, than she'd ever felt for any other man. She'd follow him to the ends of the earth if he crooked his finger.

Was it sex? Maybe. God knows the sex was powerful enough to bind her to him on that basis alone. But there was more. They might not have the same tastes but she admired him more than any other man she knew. He was brave in a way she'd never seen before, never even knew existed. Astute about the ways of the world. Observant. Intelligent.

She watched his broad back as he set the Christmas tree up in its tub and shook her head. Never in a million years would she have imagined loving a man like him. But here she was, heart thumping at the mere sight of him doing such a mundane task.

"Okay." John straightened, brushing his hands. The Christmas tree stood straight and tall. He'd chosen well. The branches were evenly spaced, a glossy forest-green pyramid. He'd centered it in the tub and it rose, tall and straight and perfect, nearly to the ceiling. "Now what?"

She walked up to him and stood on tiptoe and gave him a kiss that was pure affection. What a man. He'd never set up a Christmas tree before, yet the first time he'd done it, it was perfect. "Now...we decorate," she smiled, and placed red ribbons in his hands, hiding a smile at the look of stupefaction in his face.

She hadn't had much to choose from in the supermarket in the way of decorations, so she'd opted for simple, natural objects in a color scheme of red and white. Red ribbons, apples, popcorn.

While the turkey popped and hissed in the oven and an a cappella choir sang 'The Little Drummer Boy' and 'Do you See What I See?' they looped the red ribbons on the boughs, threaded the popcorn and hung clove-studded apples from a red ribbon bow. John was a fast learner and it didn't take him long to get up to speed, though he'd been clueless at first about trimming a Christmas tree.

"It's about balance and color." Suzanne pointed to the branch where an apple should be tied. "The decorations should be evenly spaced and you shouldn't have too many objects of the same color too closely together. Didn't you have Christmas trees when you were a kid?"

"Hmm?" John was reaching up to place a ribbon near the apex of the tree. "Nah. My mom died when I was two and my dad wouldn't have known how to decorate a tree if you'd put a gun to his head. We usually had Christmas lunch on base then went target shooting. That okay?"

He stepped back and admired his handiwork. He stood as if on a mission—broad shoulders straight, wide-legged for balance. A frown of concentration pulled his black eyebrows together. He looked exactly like a man who, against all odds, has just finished a demanding and daunting task. Attacking a well-defended enemy stronghold, maybe, or rescuing hostages held by ruthless terrorists. The warrior's stance was a little ruined by the fact that he was festooned with red ribbons. Two clove-studded apples dangled from one big hand.

She stepped back, too, and he pulled her against his side, a heavy arm around her shoulders. "I smell like a goat," he said. "Took me an hour to dig around the roots of that damned tree."

She turned her head and sniffed delicately. "A pine-scented goat," she said politely.

He snorted. "Tree turned out okay, though, didn't it? Not bad for a first effort."

The tree was pretty, she thought with satisfaction. It reached almost to the ceiling and the branches, thick and glossy, contrasted cheerily with the ribbons and apples and strands of fluffy white popcorn. The tree glowed with color. There were no store-bought ornaments on the tree, but that only made it charming, like something out of a Norman Rockwell painting.

"Pity we don't have an angel," she sighed. Her mother had a wonderful hand-made papier-machè white-and-gold angel picked up in Naples, which would have looked perfect on top of the tree.

John squeezed her shoulders and kissed the top of her head. His deep voice was quiet as he said, "You wouldn't fit on top."

Chapter Thirteen

"Is it okay?"

Suzanne was watching him anxiously, so John had to stop simply forking food into his mouth like there was no tomorrow and pretend to savor it. The food was great, considering what Suzanne had had to work with. Certainly better than his usual lukewarm can of soup and crackers up in his hideaway. But the sober truth was, he was starved. There hadn't been much time to eat these past two days and he'd worked up an appetite, what with the sex and digging up a tree. He'd have happily sucked up MREs or burnt toast, if he had to, let alone the perfectly decent meal she'd laid on. The fact that the food was good was a plus.

"It's wonderful." Reluctantly, he put his fork down and pasted an expression of sincerity on his face; when the only thing he wanted to do with his face was stuff it. "Never eaten better."

Suzanne laughed. "You are so full of it, John Huntington. Are you trying to convince me that a man who keeps an account at Comme Chez Soi can become ecstatic over frozen turkey leg pumped full of God knows what preserving agents? Give me a break."

"No, no," he protested, eyeing his forkful of turkey and baked potato with longing. "It's great, just great. Trust me." She was going to protest further, he could see it on her face. He put the fork in his mouth so he could at least be chewing while she answered.

But she only shook her head. "I guess if you compare it to raw goat, it's okay," Suzanne conceded.

She was leaning forward, beautiful face lit with amusement. Candlelight loved her face, bringing out the soft glow of her skin, highlighting the elegant curve of her cheekbones, finding hidden licks of fire in her hair. This was a woman made for candlelit dinners and romancing.

Shit. He hadn't done much of that with her. He didn't really know how. He'd always considered whatever went on between 'Hello' and 'Let's get it on' to be perfectly useless. An empty wasteland of time getting to what both parties wanted.

For the first time in his life, he could see how intriguing the journey from hello to sex could be, how pleasant it could be to smell the roses—or, rather, rose-scented skin—along the way.

His swim buddy during SEALS training, Martin Harding, had fallen in love with a philosophy student waitressing in Coronado. Marty had sent flowers and notes when they couldn't meet, which was often. SEALS training didn't allow for hearts and flowers. Marty had given up precious sleep time to see her when she got off work at 11 and to walk her home to her apartment in a rough neighborhood. And for three months he hadn't gotten laid, not once. You'd have thought that Hell Week was the last week of seminary training, for all the good it had done Marty.

At the time, John had found that amazingly stupid. All that effort and not one fuck. What was the point? Except there was a point. Marty was now married to the girl and they had three kids. And were happy.

He'd gotten everything ass-backwards with Suzanne. She was a courting kind of woman. Even a blind man could see that, could see her refinement and class. Jesus, all he'd seen were dainty curves he wanted to put his hands on and full lips he wanted to kiss. All he could think about was what her breasts tasted like and how quickly he could make her wet. All he wanted was to get into her and stay there as long as his stamina could keep him.

Even now—right now—sitting in candlelight across from her, aware that she'd somehow waved a fairy's magic wand to turn his dusty little mountain retreat into a Christmas delight, he wanted to do her. Hard and fast.

This was insane; he should have got the first fast heat of her out of his blood by now. He should be capable of settling down. But he still felt edgy around her, always semi-aroused, ready to jump her bones the instant she gave some kind of sign. Even without the sign.

He needed to slow it down, make conversation with the woman instead of remembering how soft her skin was and how it felt to be buried deep inside her. Counting the minutes between eating and when they could have sex again.

Still, even the down time was great, more intriguing than actual sex with most women.

It occurred to him, for the first time, that he might actually be in a relationship, instead of having sex. It was a novel thought, a not totally welcome one. It meant a major shift in his life, a realigning of his priorities. He wasn't entirely sure how he should feel about this.

It might even be too late. He had the uncomfortable feeling that he'd already made the leap, and his head was just now catching up.

He stole an uneasy glance at her across the candles and she responded with a smile so blinding it was like a fist to his heart.

Oh God, he was done for. Like being parachuted into a hostile foreign country with no compass and no weapons. Dead, dead, dead.

"A penny for your thoughts, John." She spooned ice cream over a huge portion of hot apple pie and handed it to him. She cut a slice about a tenth as large as his own for herself.

She definitely wouldn't want his thoughts. "I was thinking," he improvised, "that after dessert we could turn the radio on. If we can find a station with slow music, we could dance."

Suzanne looked up swiftly, eyes wide. "You dance?" She didn't have to sound so surprised. As if he said he did embroidery or collected stamps.

"No." He shrugged as she laughed. "But I figure—how hard can it be? You hold on to someone and move. Can't be harder than a HALO."

A drop of melting ice cream dotted her lip and she licked it delicately, small pink tongue wiping her lip and just like that he got a hard-on. He remembered in vivid sensory detail just how she had taken his cock into her mouth and sucked gently, tongue swirling over the head…

"What's that?"

"What's what?" He had on jeans and his blue steeler had nowhere to go. It swelled against the tight restraining material and it hurt. He couldn't concentrate.

"That thing you said—halo?"

Down boy! "HALO. High Altitude Low Opening jump. You jump out of a plane, usually at night, from 25,000 feet carrying 150 pounds of gear and don't open your 'chute till the last possible minute. Not a whole lotta fun."

"No, I can see that it wouldn't be. Dancing's a snap in comparison. So eat up your dessert, Commander. Then we'll repair from the dining room to the living room where we'll have some vin brulè. Then we can go to the ballroom for some dancing."

It was a plan he could go with, even sporting a hard-on so intense it hurt to walk. The living room—which was essentially the couch—was three steps from the dining room—which was the table—and it doubled as the ballroom. Three in one. Ah, the advantages of living in a shack.

John made it to the couch, trying not to hobble, while Suzanne brought out two steaming mugs from the kitchen. The mugs smelled of wine and Christmas. He found a station he liked on the radio and sat back.

Suzanne sat next to him and eased back into his shoulder. One hand cupping the shoulder of a beautiful woman, the other hand holding a cup of mulled wine. Life didn't get much better. They sipped.

Suzanne glanced at his lap. "You're aroused."

"Damn right." He slanted a glance at her. "I'm counting on you doing something about it."

"Mm. Later. First we dance, and then there's another Barron Christmas tradition we have to respect first."

"Does it involve red ribbons?" he asked, with interest. "I could really get into red ribbons. Oh, yeah." He warmed to the theme. "You could tie me up and put a ribbon around my—"

She punched his shoulder. "I'm not into bondage, silly." Her eyelashes fluttered. "I'm into fantasy. Like the one about the big bad soldier who kidnaps me and takes me up into his mountain lair and plies me with drink and makes love to me until I can't see straight."

"Oh, that fantasy. That's one of my specialties." It was so wonderful to see her like this, playful and flirtatious. This was the woman beneath the cool professional. This was her essence, he realized. Warm, sparkling, lively with laughter. Hidden these past days by his sex drive, which had scared her, and by fear of the damned son of a bitch who was after her. For now he'd managed to lift the veil of sadness and fear that had hid her sparkle. "We'll have to see what we can do to make every single one of your fantasies come true."

"That's nice," she sighed. Her head lay back against his arm, a blonde lock falling over his shoulder. Some kind of perfume wafted up from her, a scent guaranteed to bring a man to his knees. He let his hand drift from her shoulder to her neck, running the back of his index finger up and down the smooth length. She moved into his hand like a cat wanting to be stroked.

A ballad came on the radio, one he was familiar with because it had been playing in all the bars while he'd trained. His brain was imprinted with it. He rose from the sofa, pulling her up, wrapping his arm around her. "I'm willing to break my back fulfilling your fantasies, honey, but first I need to have this dance."

She slipped gracefully into his arms, already moving, following his pathetically simple two-step with ease. They swayed and he hazarded a simple dip. When she came up, laughing and flushed, he felt like Fred Astaire.

He buried his nose in her hair and turned with her in his arms, the music and her perfume filling his head. He still had a hard-on and she had to feel it, but it was okay. They were going to make love soon; both of them knew it. It could wait another minute or two. He was going to make sure this time it was lovemaking and not fucking. No wall jobs, no taking her from behind. It was going to be in a bed and he was going to be on top and it was going to be slow and soft. Even if it killed him.

Her body fit so neatly against his. He turned and she followed gracefully, breasts brushing his chest, legs sliding against his. Dancing was something else he'd underrated. He'd always considered it a second-rate form of foreplay. Why do it, when you could have the real thing?

It was foreplay, but pleasant in its own right. The music filled his head, a slow liquid beat that seemed to pulse in time with his heart. Suzanne was light and graceful in his arms, and she filled his head, too, the scent and the feel of her. He tightened his grip and she moved even closer, part of the music, part of him. It felt as if every movement he made was made with her, as if she were an extension of himself.

It was so easy to lose yourself this way, to be one with the night and the music and the woman. If he was already in a relationship, and he'd discovered he liked dancing, then there would be more of this in his future. He knew he was a goner when that prospect didn't fill him with dread.

He brought their entwined hands up and tilted her head back with his thumb. His head lowered. Suzanne stopped swaying. She disengaged their hands and placed her palm on his chest. "Not just yet, soldier. There's something more we have to do."

Whatever it was, she wasn't refusing him. The warmth in her eyes as she looked at him was clear. She lifted on tiptoe, pressed a kiss to his mouth, then took him by the hand. In passing, she picked up two candles, a box of matches, and her coat. He helped her on with the coat and she led him to the door.

Outside, the night had turned clear as glass and icy cold. There was no cloud cover and, so far from any light pollution, the stars were thick and bright overhead, the Milky Way a creamy rope across the sky. They stood on the porch under the star-bright night sky. Still and fresh, it was like the first night of a new life, where the new world would be bright and clean.

He held Suzanne, as fresh and beautiful as the night, tightly by his side. The match flared and Suzanne lit a candle, placing the other in his hand.

They watched the candle burn for a moment, the flame rising bright and straight in the still air. "In my family, we have a tradition," Suzanne said quietly. "We all gather on Christmas Eve for a late supper. When I was small, there was my mom and dad and me, plus aunts and uncles and both sets of grandparents. After dinner, we'd listen to music or play charades until midnight. Then we'd all troop outdoors holding a candle. My father would make a little speech about how blessed we were to be with our loved ones and what he hoped for the world in the coming year. He would always end by saying 'peace'. He'd light his candle, and light my mother's candle with his. She'd light mine. The light was passed from person to person and we'd all say 'peace'. It was like we were summoning peace from the spirit of Christmas." She looked up at him and he saw the glimmer of tears in her eyes. She lowered her candle to his, her flame igniting his. It flared, and then settled to burn steadily. "Peace, John", she whispered.

Peace.

He hadn't had much of it in his lifetime, hadn't missed it, and hadn't even looked for it. But peace moved through him in a powerful surge, warming him. He now recognized that was what he'd felt like a punch to the heart on opening the door to his shack this afternoon to a little wonderland of beauty and grace. Peace. And a sense that he'd come home.

Peace and homecoming, for a man who was a warrior and who'd never had a home. In the space of a few days, this remarkable woman had created two homes for him and filled them with peace.

"Peace, Suzanne." He gave her promise back to her and bent down.

They kissed, lightly, holding their candles in the chill night air, under a million stars. John moved his mouth on hers, keeping it gentle because that's what he felt in his heart. The long, slow glide of lips and tongue, the sigh of breath meeting breath, heartbeat to heartbeat, that was peace.

John set the candles on the railing, where they burned brightly, side by side. He watched them a moment, then bent to gently blow them out. He turned back to Suzanne. Their lips met again and he bent to lift her in his arms, holding her high against his heart, kissing her as he carried her inside. Music from the radio provided a counterpoint to the drumbeat in his head. He considered, briefly, turning it off, but it seemed appropriate to lay Suzanne across his bed to the strains of 'Joy to the World.'

Joy. John couldn't help but smile down at her in joy. With no sense of hurry, he stripped, his gaze locked with hers. He was naked in seconds and she could clearly see what she did to him. Part of him—the old John—wanted to jump on top of her and enter her fast. She was ripe and ready, sighing, legs moving restlessly. Rip pants and panties off her and put it in.

That was the old John. The new one wanted to savor each step, each slow unveiling. This John bent to take her shoes and socks off, slowly. Right foot, left foot. He held her foot for a moment, admiring the elegant arch, the subtle play of tendon and muscle. He wanted to see more, see those long, slender legs gleam in the shadowy darkness. The rasp of the zipper, the hiss of material as he pulled pants and panties down and off and there she was. Naked from the waist down, covered only by a soft cherry-red sweater. He picked her right foot up again and lifted it to his mouth.

It exposed her. Enough light filtered in from the living room to show the folds of her sex, open and already glistening. His cock came away from his stomach in a surge and lengthened.

"John. Look at me. I'm ready." Suzanne lifted her other leg then let it fall to the side. She was completely open to him. "Come to me now," she whispered.

He didn't answer, couldn't. Words choked in his throat. All he could do was to bend and kiss her foot, nibbling, listening to the catch of her breath as he suckled her toes, one by one. He kneeled on the bed, watching her eyes. Everything he did to her tonight had to be pure liquid pleasure for her, joy heaped on joy. Her eyes would tell him what worked and what didn't.

Light nips along the arch of her foot, a fingertip running from ankle to thigh worked. Her sighs rose in the room. He meant for there to be moans and then screams before he was done.

Lips, then fingers, trailed up her legs. That worked, too. He placed his hands on the inside of her knees and pressed them open, gently. Her sex unfolded like petals of roses, wet with dew.

His thoughts surprised him, even shocked him. He'd never had these images in his head before, ever. Sex was sex, period. Getting your rocks off was fun while it lasted, but not part of the important business of life. This…this was different. And important as hell.

"John." Her voice was a languid sigh and it raised the hairs along his forearms. The red sweater, molded to her firm breasts, rose and fell. She was breathing rapidly, almost panting. And he lost it.

He knew—he knew—what he should do next. He should pull that sweater off her slowly, get rid of the bra and lick and suck her breasts. She had small nipples that grew even smaller and rock hard when she was turned on. She liked it when he sucked hard and even when he bit lightly. She'd bucked the first time he did that, as if no one had ever bit her nipple before. He loved the thought that he was doing things to her no man had ever done before.

His hand would move down and he'd enter her with one finger, then when she softened up a bit, he'd put in a second. He'd spread his fingers slowly, getting her ready for him. She'd come fast this way and her cunt would pull at his fingers. He knew how to keep it going for a while, make her cry with her orgasm.

When she stilled, he'd slide down her, kissing her stomach along the way, and finally taste her, something he hadn't got around to yet. Going down on women wasn't something he did often, only when he got tired of having his cock in the woman and by that time he was usually bored enough to call it off.

He knew Suzanne would be somehow different. Spicy and warm and exciting. So yeah, he'd bury his tongue in her until she came again. Whenever she came for the second time, she pulled harder and it lasted longer. While she was coming, he'd bury his cock in her, thrusting in time with her contractions, keeping it up until she went into meltdown.

Yeah, that's what he should have done.

What he actually did was climb on top of her, open her with his fingers and thrust in, hard. She gasped and squirmed under him. He could feel her, frantically trying to adjust to him, to his size and length.

He'd skipped the extensive foreplay; the least he could do was stay still while she adjusted. Though he wanted to start moving—hard—he lay still on top of her, face buried in her neck. His back was tense and his ass tight as he held himself deep inside her. She was softening slowly, by degrees. Her legs opened wider and she hooked them around his, sleek and slim and strong. When Suzanne pushed her pelvis up against him, rocking gently, he let out his breath. Oh yeah. She was ready.

How could he keep from fucking her blind? He wanted some control, some way to keep it gentle, for the first time. As he held himself still, the buzzing in his head quieted enough to hear the radio, still playing soft music. That's what he'd do. He'd make love to her to a slow beat. That should give him a modicum of control.

The strains of 'Amazing Grace' filtered in, and he began to move slowly, in time with the music. A leisurely, languid in and out. Suzanne sighed in his ear, giving him goose bumps, rising to meet his slow strokes.

John slipped his hands under her hips to pull her more tightly against him on the downstroke. The music was working fine, helping him keep a slippery clutch on control. His mouth fastened on the skin behind her ear, where a hickey wouldn't show, while his hips pumped in measured strokes.

Suzanne moaned and started shaking under him. His back was bathed with sweat from the effort of keeping from pumping hard and fast into her. He felt raw and open, fighting to keep the reins of control from slithering out of his grasp. The music helped, a little, but then it stopped and a smooth baritone voice started talking. The news.

Suzanne gasped and stilled. When she started coming, he'd be a goner. He waited for her contractions to start and for him to lose control. He jolted with surprise when her legs slipped down onto the mattress and she pushed at his shoulders.

"Get off me, John." What? "Get off me now."

She pushed again and he reared up and pulled out of her, his cock red and inflamed and wet. He was puzzled and frustrated. What the fuck?

Suzanne was sitting up, shivering, reaching for the covers. She pushed her hair back out of her eyes.

"What the hell are you doing? Why did you stop me?" John didn't even try to keep the anger out of his voice when he saw from her body language that the sex was over. She was already reaching down beside the bed for panties and pants. In seconds she was dressed and standing. When she looked down at him, there was nothing in her face to show they'd just been making love. Her breathing was loud, chest rising and falling, eyes wide with emotion. When John realized that emotion was fear, he rolled off the bed and started walking towards her.

"Dear sweet God in heaven." Her voice was shocked, breathless. "I think I know what's been going on and who's after me." She drew in a deep, shaky breath. "I think I witnessed a murder."

Chapter Fourteen

The trembling wouldn't stop. Suzanne put a hand to her mouth, and then wrapped her arms around herself. She was cold down to her core. She looked helplessly at John. He was standing against the open doorway, his big naked body outlined by the light. She could see the gleam of his erect penis, still wet from her.

It had happened so quickly. One moment, she'd been tensing against his penis, feeling the waves of an orgasm building and the next, she'd been pushing at John's shoulders, eager to get him off her. Just like that, a switch had been thrown.

She could still hear the smooth baritone of the announcer's voice. She wouldn't have paid any attention, normally, but it had been so lovely to feel John's body moving in hers, while the graceful notes of 'Amazing Grace' moved in her head. When the music stopped, she was still listening.

"This is Loren Bannister with some breaking news. The brutally beaten body of a Portland woman, Marissa Carson, was found today. The authorities say she was murdered sometime in the afternoon of the 22nd of December. The woman lay unnoticed in her apartment until a neighbor, returning from a business trip, noticed her dog barking constantly. The neighbor called the police.

Marissa Carson's husband, businessman Peter Carson, who has just returned from a two-week vacation in Aruba, is cooperating with the authorities."

John had pulled on his jeans, leaving them unzipped. He walked barefoot towards her, clutching her arms in a grip that almost, but not quite, hurt. He shook her. "What's going on, Suzanne? What the hell do you mean—you saw a murder?"

Suzanne opened her mouth, but felt a sob about to come out. She snapped her mouth closed and shook her head. I will not cry, I will not cry, I will not cry. It was a mantra in her head. She swallowed heavily, bile rising in her throat. "I haven't seen a TV here. Do you have one?"

His jaws clenched, but he didn't blink at the change of subject. "No."

"Oh." Suzanne thought furiously. She needed to know— "Do you have a computer with internet access?"

He studied her for a long moment, then gave a sharp nod of his head. "Follow me."

Follow me sounded odd when applied to a tiny shack. Still, she followed his broad back into the living room then watched, astounded, as he moved a throw rug aside, put his thumb to a screen and a piece of the floor simply rose up on silent hydraulics. It was connected to a steel ladder angling downwards.

He had another room downstairs, and she hadn't even suspected. He took the lead and she followed him down the rungs of the ladder to stand under a harsh neon light, blinking. The room's perimeters were the perimeters of the whole shack, so it was fairly large. It was bristling with electronics, blue steel, brushed aluminum. Suzanne didn't know much about computer technology but she knew enough to realize that she was looking at tens of thousands of dollars of top-of-the-line equipment. No wonder upstairs had felt so bleak and abandoned. The heart of the house was here, gleaming metal, blinking lights, the hum of technology.

John was unfolding a sleek ultra thin laptop. He punched a few keys and with a beep, the screen was filled with the logo of a famous search engine. He looked at her, waiting. His expression was still.

"Can you find a news site, something local?" Suzanne doubted whether the murder would have made any of the major news sites, like CNN. It had to be local.

John nodded and logged onto an unfamiliar site. It had what she wanted, though.

"Click here." She pointed at the screen and John obeyed. She was glad he wasn't plying her with questions, because she wasn't sure how cogent she could be. A new page blinked on and there it was—Portland Woman Bludgeoned to Death. Suzanne pointed at the screen again. He clicked and up came a studio portrait of Marissa, which she recognized, from having seen it in Marissa's living room.

"I was in that woman's apartment the afternoon she was murdered. She was a client. I might be the last person to see her alive." She reached past John to scroll down to the photograph of the husband, Peter Carson, being interviewed at the airport on his arrival from Aruba. "Except for him. He wasn't in Aruba, John. He was in Portland, and I saw him going into Marissa's house the afternoon she was killed." She laid a hand on his massive shoulder and squeezed. "He killed her."

* * * * *

Fuck.

John stared at the computer screen. He was used to tactical and strategic thinking and he saw it all, plain as the chart of a Civil War battlefield. He saw every move and what every move entailed. He saw the steps that had to be taken and the consequences.

He also saw that this was the end of her life, as she knew it. And his. He leaned back, feeling old and tired, knowing what was ahead.

"Peter Carson." He looked up at Suzanne. She was pale, a few lines of stress etched on her forehead. There'd be more—lots more—before this was over. "What do you know about him? And about his wife?"

Suzanne took one of his camp chairs, unfolded it, and sat down. "I don't know Peter Carson at all. I never met him, except for the 22nd, as I told you. His wife is—was—a client of mine. I was called in to redecorate her home and we spent some time together going over the design. She was difficult, always changing her mind, so I probably saw her a few times more than I would have a normal client. She wasn't a particularly nice woman. I never saw her husband. I just saw photographs of him everywhere in Marissa's apartment. Or rather…his pictures were everywhere until the last time I was there. On the 22nd. The day she died."

"All the photographs were gone?"

"Yes. And Marissa was…I don't know. Agitated. She couldn't sit still. She kept making comments and hints, and then looking at me as if I should understand what she was saying. The only thing I really grasped was that she thought she was going to come into some money. A lot of money."

It couldn't have been clearer to John if he'd had a diagram drawn for him. "She was blackmailing him. She was hoping for a big divorce settlement otherwise she'd go public with what she knew about his business dealings. Or go to the police. It doesn't matter. The point is she was going to expose him unless he paid her."

"Expose what?"

John sighed and stood up. She might as well know. While he talked, he was planning. In fifteen minutes they could be packed and out of here. What would be a good place to fly out of? Not Portland, not Seattle. Maybe Boise. They could make it to Boise by morning. Abandon the Yukon with another set of false plates. He had two sets of false identities here, but not for a woman. He had to get them to a small town outside St. Louis where a master forger he knew could get a new set of papers for Suzanne. They'd lay low somewhere in the Midwest for a few weeks, then take the next leg of the journey.

There was a tug of regret at having to abandon the shack. He had a lot of good material up here. An even greater tug of regret at having to give up his new company. But he'd learned the hard way not to dwell on regrets. This was the way it was.

"Paul Carson isn't a businessman, honey," he said as he started climbing the ladder. She was following him up, puzzled. He headed into the bedroom and pulled his duffel bag out. "He's the point man on the West Coast for the Russian Mafia. He's got his hand in all sorts of nasty stuff, including human trafficking. He's also under suspicion of counterfeiting airplane parts. You remember the crash of Flight 901?"

Suzanne nodded, wide-eyed.

"The FBI traced the sale of defective washers to Carson, to a company he owned, but they couldn't prove it. Not something that would hold up in court. Their inside witness was found hanging from a meat hook. The guy's ruthless as hell. Get your stuff together."

"All right." Without arguing, Suzanne quietly set about packing her bag. Good girl, he thought. "Do you want to tell Bud that we're coming?"

He just stared at her. Hadn't she heard what he'd just said? "No, of course not. We're not going to Bud, we're going to disappear. This is worse than I thought. We'll have to go underground and reappear somewhere else, as someone else, far away. I have a couple of false documents and I know where to get more. I was thinking we could relocate to the Keys, if you like the beach. Or Canada, if you're hung up on the cold. Can you step it up a little, honey? I want to get going as soon as possible. I thought we'd drive to Boise, catch a flight out of there."

Suzanne was holding a shirt bunched in her hands, staring. "I don't understand. Why on earth would I want to go to the Keys? Or Canada? Or Boise? I need to get down to Bud. Or—or the FBI. Or someone. Didn't you hear what I said, John? I witnessed a murder. Or at least, my testimony puts the husband at Marissa's house at the right time. If he was lying about being there, then he must be the killer."

Now he was angry. Good. Anger kept the fear away. Anger made sure he didn't think too closely about Paul Carson gunning for Suzanne. Getting his hands on her. Carson was utterly ruthless and would take her apart.

John strode over to Suzanne, ripped the shirt out of her hands and glared down at her. He went toe to toe with her, so she was forced to tilt her head back to look at him. He knew how intimidating he could be and he used that deliberately now, utterly without remorse.

She looked up at him and he made sure she was aware that he outweighed her by 100 pounds and was almost a foot taller than she was.

"Now listen up, Suzanne, I'm going to say this once. We don't have much time and every minute I spend explaining the situation to you is a minute lost. You are not going to testify against Paul Carson. The man is a murderer, and was one long before he offed his wife. If you testify against him, your life is over. He will gun you down before you make it to the courthouse to testify before the grand jury. If he doesn't manage that, and maybe, just maybe he won't because the FBI will put you in a safe house and guard you 24/7, you can bet Carson will pull out all the stops to get to you before you testify in court. Every hired gun in the country will have a photograph of you and a contract in his pocket. The FBI will sit on you until your trial and you just might live till then. Maybe. But afterwards you'll go straight into Witness Protection where you'll wind up a waitress in Bumfuck, Nebraska for the rest of what remains of your life. And Paul Carson's in prison with lots of time to think of ways of getting to you. He's got more money than a third world country and a small army of goons and he won't quit. It's a question of time. So those are your choices—being dumped by the Marshall's Service on some windblown prairie to live out your life—your very short life—in some dead-end job, completely alone and always looking over your shoulder. Oh, and if you go into the Program forget about ever seeing your parents or me or your friends or Portland again for the rest of your life."

His voice had risen. Now he took a deep breath and lowered it. "Or you can come with me. I know how to make us disappear. I can set us up in another part of the country, or even abroad, with completely new identities and I can do it better and faster than the Witness Protection people. We can live quietly and even well. If we keep our noses clean, make sure our new identities are deep enough, you could even have a low-key job as a decorator in five or ten years' time. So those are your choices, Suzanne. Waitressing on the prairie and living alone or coming with me."

He could feel his jaws clench, holding back the fear and the rage.

"Which will it be?"

*****

The Midnight Man was back. That was Suzanne's first thought. He'd come back the moment John had seen the name Paul Carson on the screen. John's eyes were the color of blued steel. Just as cold and just as hard.

What he'd said…her mind whirled. He'd already made the leap forward into her choices while she was still struggling with the implications of what she'd seen and what it meant.

Run away. It sounded enticing, especially with John Huntington by her side. Go to some tropical island somewhere, calling themselves Patsy and Steven Smith and eat coconuts and down drinks with little umbrellas. It beat waitressing in Nebraska, all alone. She wouldn't have to keep looking over her shoulder, not with John by her side. He'd take care of her in all ways. Disappearing with John was the more attractive solution, no doubt about it.

There was only one thing wrong.

A man would get away with murder.

John was standing too close to her, well within what she considered her personal space, and he was glaring at her. It was as if he could will her into escaping with him. Stepping into a void and stepping out again somewhere else, someone else. God, was the thought tempting.

What John hadn't said, hadn't mentioned in any way, was the sacrifice he would be making. He hadn't said that, in making his offer, he was willing to throw away a lifetime of hard work. Jettison his new company. Be unable to use his military background as reference. He'd do all that for her, without question and without asking anything in return.

Midnight Man might be a harsh warrior, but he'd proven that he had a soft spot for her, that he was willing to sacrifice everything for her. Tears burned her eyes.

She sat down on the side of the bed and tugged at his arm until he sat too. She could feel him vibrate with his desire to get moving, but the question was—in which direction?

"Which will it be?" he'd asked. And she answered him.

"John," she said quietly. "Listen to me. Listen carefully." She put her hand over his. It was pale and slender, almost half the size of his but she knew it was as if she'd put a stake through his hand. He was frozen in place by her hand on his. "Do you know, I admire your courage tremendously. It's the kind of courage I simply don't have." He started to speak and she placed a finger across his lips. "Shh. Hear me out. As I was saying, I'm not brave at all; you're not going to catch me with a gun in my hand, going after the bad guys. But I can do this, John. No, I have to do this. Paul Carson probably killed his wife. If he did, he has to go to jail. If I refuse to testify, I'm condoning murder. If I refuse to testify, our system crashes. I must do this. I must. It's my duty as a citizen. I am honor-bound to do it."

His hand tensed under hers and he bowed his head, broad shoulders slumping. Suzanne knew she'd used the one argument he couldn't refute. He was a former military officer. Duty and honor were bred in his blood and bone.

John rose, slowly, as if he were an old man. Their eyes met. This moment changed everything. He was about to set in motion a process that would separate them forever.

The tears that had been threatening were now flowing down her cheeks, but she met his gaze head-on. She wasn't backing down, and he knew it.

John reached for something in his duffel bag. A cell phone. He punched in some numbers.

"Bud. John here. Listen up. There've been developments."

* * * * *

It happened fast. Within twenty minutes, they were heading back down the dirt road, which led to a secondary road feeding into the highway. John had made an appointment with Bud and the federal agents at a spot about fifty miles away.

Suzanne knew what was going to happen, because John had explained it carefully, eyes blank, face hard, no expression at all in his deep voice. Midnight Man.

She would be taken into custody by federal agents. It was a federal case—trafficking and smuggling—and they'd been on Paul Carson's tail for the past fifteen years. Bud Morrison would accompany her. John had explained that Bud would be there as 'liaison' between Portland PD and what he called 'the feebs', but she'd heard him on the phone arguing, insisting on Bud's presence. Bud would be there, at least in the beginning, because she knew Bud and would be reassured by a familiar face.

John was doing his best to protect her even when she would be taken beyond his reach.

The FBI would 'debrief' her, which was a fancy term for questioning her. She would be taken to a safe house until the

District Attorney could put together a case for a grand jury. After testifying, she would be kept in another safe house until the trial. The FBI's job stopped then. The U.S. Marshal's Service would take over, giving her a new identity and placing her in the most anonymous setting they could devise. And that was where she would spend the rest of her life. In hiding.

She'd never see her parents again. Technically, they weren't supposed to know anything about what had happened to her. To them, she would have disappeared off the face of the earth. But John had promised her he'd let them know, discreetly.

Taking care of her, again.

She'd never see John again. Scant hours after realizing she loved the man, he'd be taken from her forever. There would be no other man for her. How could there be? Having known John, having loved him, she couldn't even contemplate loving another man. No other man could ever measure up.

Her life was ending with each mile the SUV ate up, bleeding away just as surely as the lifeblood bled out of someone who'd been in a fatal accident.

She blinked back tears. She didn't want to cry, she wanted to see everything, grasp every second of this life before it ended. The night was still, the stars brilliant in the icy sky. A beautiful night to be the last night of her old life. Suzanne shivered and huddled more deeply into the comfort of John's sheepskin jacket, which he'd insisted she put on. It smelled of him, a musky male scent she'd carry with her forever.

His profile was hard and clean, the only signs of tension the muscles jumping in his jaw. Suzanne eyed him hungrily, wanting to hoard images of him to add to her pitiful stockpile. A few days. They'd only had a few days. Despite her best efforts, a lone tear coursed down her cheek.

With a vicious curse, John wrenched the steering wheel and brought the SUV to a sudden halt by the side of the road. He stared ahead, breathing hard, and then lowered his head to the steering wheel.

"Fuck." His voice was the merest whisper. He turned his head, eyes bleak. "I can't do this, Suzanne. I can't give you up to them."

"You have to." Her heart was cracking open. There was no question of holding back the tears now. "You have no choice."

They moved at the same time. She launched herself into his arms at the same moment he opened them to haul her onto his lap.

They kissed, violently, hungrily, a meeting of lips and tongue and tears. Her tears. He wasn't crying but she could feel his muscles tense as rocks beneath her hands.

He was holding the back of her head tightly, while eating at her mouth, as if he could fuse them at the lips. His tongue was deep in her mouth. She'd take the taste of him to her grave.

"Don't go, goddammit. Stay with me." His voice was thick and gravelly. The words came out between biting kisses. "I. Can't. Stand. To. Let. You. Go."

His hard hands moved up under her sweater. He didn't bother loosening her bra. He just shoved it up together with the sweater and bent her over his arm. Cupping his hand around her breast, he held it for his mouth, opened wide over her nipple. He suckled her hard, biting and sucking, pulling at her with the strength of his mouth. Just like that, she surged into climax. She had no idea she was ready; the orgasm—a hard, tight one that left her unsatisfied—took her completely by surprise.

She could see his cheeks working on her breasts and had a flash of an alternate future. She could see herself on a sofa with John sitting beside her. She was holding their child, feeding at her breast. A child who would never be born.

With shaking hands, crying with desperation, Suzanne sat up and fumbled with the snap of his jeans. She needed him inside her more than she needed her next breath. She rarely took the lead with a man, and never with John. But now, right now, she'd have clawed her way through concrete to get to him.

Their hands tangled as they raced to unbutton, unzip, open. She toed her own shoes off, and pulled her pants and panties down and off. She left the sweater and jacket on. No need to get naked. All they needed was the bare minimum uncovered, for him to…

Ah!

There he was, enormous and hard as stone. She whimpered as she put her hands on him, feeling the steely strength. That penis had been the source of such delight for her, but now wasn't about pleasure or sensuality. Now was about being connected with him in the most elemental way possible. Now was about feeling him inside her, moving, a part of her.

She opened her labia herself and positioned herself over him. Though she'd already had an orgasm, she still found it difficult to give him passage. But she persisted, even when it became slightly painful, because the thought of not having him inside her was unbearable. Finally she was straddling him, completely impaled. His rough pubic hairs scratched her sensitive inner thighs. Her vagina adjusted itself slowly to him. She imagined that if things had worked out differently and they could have lived together, they would have made love so often she would eventually be permanently stretched to accommodate the size of his penis.

Straddling his lap this way, her face was on a level with his. It was dark, but she knew his face well. He was suffering as much as she was. Midnight Man was gone; in his place was a man at the end of his emotional tether.

It was unbearably intimate this way, feeling him deeply buried inside her while watching his eyes. Her hand reached underneath his sweater to touch his chest, running her fingers over the thick mat of hair. She rested her hands over his massive pectorals and could feel his heart thundering under her right hand. His breath washed her face.

Suzanne rotated her hips around the smooth hard column.

She searched his eyes as she began a tentative rocking motion. "I'm sorry I'm on the pill. I wish I weren't. I'd give anything if I could become pregnant right now, this instant. At least I'd have your child with me for the rest of my life."

His eyes flared and the penis within her lengthened, thickened. It was so amazing to see and feel at the same time his reaction to her words.

His big hands cupped her backside, sliding her even more closely on to him. "If you were pregnant," he growled, "no way would I let anyone have you. I'd kidnap you if I had to."

"John." Her voice broke. She could barely get any sound out through the constriction in her chest. Her throat hurt with unshed tears. He began thrusting, slowly, and she was sure he could see the effects of his movements in her eyes. "I am going to miss you…so much." She said the words against his mouth, rocking up and down against his lips with the force of his thrusts.

John lifted one hand to hold the back of her head. He kissed her, hard, biting her lips. "I want you to remember this," he gasped, his penis working strong and hard and fast now. "I want you to remember the taste of my mouth on yours, how my cock feels in you. I want you to walk away with my come still inside you. I want you to remember…this." He thrust upward so hard she gasped, and slid right over the edge. He kept moving inside her through her orgasm as she rocked and shook and cried. When she lay quiescent against him, wrung out, he held her tightly against him as he moved into his own orgasm. He muffled his shout against her hair, but it was still loud in the dark cab.

They sat quietly together for a long time; Suzanne's legs still straddling his hips, sweat drying. Still connected.

He held her tightly and she rubbed her face against his neck. Tears pooled in her eyes, but she didn't cry. She was all cried out and tears wouldn't help now, anyway.

She was frantically trying to commit every second to memory. The feel of his penis—barely softened by the orgasm—inside her, his breath against her hair, his hand running up and down her back beneath her sweater.

Suzanne wanted to stay like this forever, but eventually John shifted and sighed. "We'd better be going." He kissed her hair and lifted her away from him. She rummaged on the floor for her panties, found them, and then pulled on her slacks. It was easier for John. All he had to do was lift his hips to hitch his pants up, then zip up.

Suzanne knew how disheveled she looked. Knew her hair was uncombed, knew her face was covered in tear tracks, knew her lips were swollen from his biting kisses. She smelled of sex. She could feel his semen between her thighs. She knew all of that, knew she would be meeting federal agents who would take one look at her and know. She couldn't find it in her to care.

John turned the ignition. "It's time," he said. His voice was low and steady. She looked at him, at his carefully expressionless face and wanted to weep.

Midnight Man was back.

* * * * *

They were waiting where they'd said they'd be—two unmarked cars, which screamed FBI and Bud's PD-issue Crown Victoria. John had made sure that Bud would be around to ease Suzanne's way, at least for the first few days. Suzanne was going to be scared and lonely, kept under lock and key. It was an obscenity, the idea of a woman as lovely, as vibrant as Suzanne locked in, her life essentially over. He needed to know Bud would be there for her, at least in the beginning.

The feebs emerged from their cars before he finished braking. There were four agents. John couldn't see the faces very clearly, but then he didn't have to. They were essentially the same man. They were dressed in the same clothes, were more or less the same height and had all read the same operation manual.

Bud got out of his car and came to stand beside the agents, towering over them. White plumes came from everyone's mouth. The temperature had dropped below zero.

John propelled Suzanne forward and she moved within the cone of light cast by his headlights. He could see the eyes of the agents widen with surprise at the sight of her, and then shutter down. He trusted their professionalism, knew that, technically, Suzanne would not only be safe with them, but would be safe from them.

That didn't mean they weren't men. They'd have to be without a pulse not to react to her.

She wasn't as polished-looking as when he'd first met her. Her clothes were rumpled and her makeup was gone. Her hair needed combing. But she was a heart-stopper, a potent mix of class and sex. A magnet for the male eye.

The instant they got a close look at her, they'd know. It wasn't just the bee-stung lips or love-bite he'd just given her. It was the way she walked, moved. She was a well-loved woman who'd just had sex and it showed.

Bud came forward. He put his arm around her and bent down to talk to her. She nodded at his words.

John couldn't hear what Bud was saying but it didn't matter. It would be some bullshit meant to reassure her that everything would be all right.

It wouldn't.

"Okay," one of the feebs said, "let's go."

Suzanne turned back to him, eyes glistening. She was ready to break and run to him for a final embrace. John could read it in her body language. He stepped back. If he took her in his arms, he'd never let her go. Suzanne stared at him, then turned when an agent touched her elbow. One last lingering glance at him, and she slid into the back seat of the lead car. The agents got in and started the cars.

Bud was left standing, looking at him. They stared at each other and John could see that Bud understood.

A minute later, John watched the taillights of the cars as they topped a hill and disappeared.

John turned back to the SUV and took off in a hurry. He knew what he had to do and he had to do it fast.

The hunter stalks his prey. The prey is alert, but the hunter is stealthy and patient. The hunter is an expert and has done this before, has stalked and killed humans before. Humans leave spoor and have habits, just as animal prey do.

The hunter has been lying here for four days and four nights, sipping frugally from a canteen, eating nothing, eyes glued to the forty-power spotting scope with night vision.

The hunter has mud and greasepaint on his face, is buried belly-down in the root pocket of a giant oak and is wearing a ghillie suit designed to meld into a wintry Pacific Northwest landscape. He smells like an animal, which is good. The other animals in the forest give him a wide berth because they recognize him for what he is—a large and dangerous predator. He is in killing mode and the other animals sense that.

Below, in the valley, is a large limestone villa, surrounded by guards. The hunter finds the guards with their elaborate security watches and the thick surrounding walls topped with barbed wire ridiculous. From his vantage point, anyone who steps out of the villa steps right into his crosshairs.

The shot is already lined up, elevation has been calculated. When the prey is in the crosshairs, windage will be factored in. The hunter knows how to do this, supremely well.

The hunter's comrades have given him intelligence. The prey is in the villa, secluded and alone, except for the guards. The comrades have given the hunter watch times, schedules, a list of enemy firepower and their promise to help him. But the hunter has chosen to act alone. This is his fight, his war. He stands alone. If he has to die, he will die alone.

He waits, day after day, night after night.

At midnight on the fourth night, a night so windless the hunter knows he could drive tacks into a target, the prey steps out to stand for a moment. He is tall, blond, handsome, with cold features clearly visible in the night scope. He pauses for a moment, looking around, feeling secure. Foolishly secure.

He is surrounded by walls and guards. He doesn't know they are as nothing. He bends to light a cigarette and the green flare in the night vision goggles ruins the hunter's vision for a moment. He waits.

He waits for the prey to pull on his cigarette, blow out a leisurely plume of smoke, which dissipates slowly in the cold still air. Waits for the prey to exchange pleasantries with the guards. Waits for him to pull in a breath of the pristine mountain air, secure in his safety and immunity.

And it is then, when the prey crushes the cigarette beneath his heel, having taken a last, secure glance at his rich and safe kingdom, starting to turn back inside, it is then that the hunter strikes.

Something was happening in the living room. Male voices were raised in excitement. The phone rang constantly. Suzanne debated briefly going in to see what was going on, but she didn't really care. In the four days and four nights she'd been locked up in the safe house, she'd learned to turn her emotions off, otherwise she'd have gone mad.

There were no windows and she knew the time of day only because of her wristwatch and the small TV in her room.

She didn't even know where she was. She'd been flown to a small airport, but they'd been met by a car out on the tarmac, in the General Aviation section and she couldn't see the name of the airport. What did it matter? Wherever she was, she wasn't free. Wherever she was, John wasn't with her.

The time had seemed interminable. Bud had stayed with her the first three days but had had to leave yesterday.

Thank God the debriefing had finally ended. She had told her story over and over, to agent after agent. Finally, they had just left her alone. From the conversations of the agents looking after her, she understood that the grand jury arraignment would be soon. Then there would be another safe house. The trial. Then the new life would begin.

She leafed her magazine, not bothering to read the articles. Her eyes blurred with tiredness. She'd cried herself to sleep night after night, astounded that she had so many tears in her. Last night had been no exception. Now it was morning and she had another endless day to get through.

At some point in the future, the tears would stop. They must. Soon, she hoped.

The door to her bedroom opened and she looked up. Through the door into the living room, she could see at least ten FBI agents, instead of the usual four. The phone rang again, the fifth time in half an hour. What was going on?

She'd never seen the man who walked in before, but he was a clone of the others. They were all the same: medium height, dark cheap suit, utterly humorless. "Ms. Barron? May I have a word with you?"

Oh God, not another debriefing. She put her magazine down. "Yes?"

"Out here, please." He held the door open, gesturing towards the living room.

Suppressing a sigh, Suzanne stood up and followed the man out the door. The conversations going on stopped when she walked into the room. All eyes turned to her. What was going on?

The man took her elbow and led her to a chair. He sat down next to her. "Ms. Barron, I'm Special Agent Alan Crowley and I'm in charge of the Carson case. There have been…developments. An unusual set of circumstances." He stopped and looked at her as if expecting a response.

"Yes?" she said, finally.

"Ms. Barron, we've received word that several hours ago, Paul Carson was shot and killed."

Suzanne stared at him, uncomprehending. "What?"

"An unknown assailant, a sniper, shot Paul Carson through the head. Which means there is no longer a federal case against him. Which means, Ms. Barron, that you are free to go."

"I—" Suzanne looked around, at the vast display of FBI power, the safe house, back to Special Agent Crowley. "I'm free to go? I'm…safe?"

He sighed. "Yes. You're not a threat to the people Paul Carson was working for. You were a threat to him, personally. Now that he's been…taken out, no one would come after you. They'd just be creating more problems for themselves. Our street informers have assured us of this. We wouldn't be letting you go if we weren't certain that you're safe. So you're free to go."

Free to go. Free. To. Go. Suzanne blinked, wondering if her exhaustion was playing tricks with her mind. She opened her mouth to ask Special Agent Crowley to repeat what he'd said when the front door of the apartment opened and Bud stepped in.

Oh, how nice. Bud had come to take her home. She smiled at Bud and then froze when Bud moved aside. There was another man behind Bud, just as tall, just as broad-shouldered but with close-cropped black hair and gunmetal eyes. The hair on the nape of her neck rose.

Suzanne stood up slowly, shaking. Oh, God, she thought she'd never see him again. She wanted to call his name, but her throat was closed. Her legs could barely hold her up.

Suzanne looked at him hungrily. He looked leaner. Had he somehow lost weight in the past few days? Lines of exhaustion clawed his beard-shadowed face and he was filthy. He had the look of a wild animal about him.

She took one step, then two, and then ran into John's arms. His arms closed around her fiercely, and she broke into sobs.

"We won't ever find the weapon, will we?" Special Agent Crowley asked behind her.

John's eyes were cold as he looked at the agent. "I don't know what the hell you're talking about."

He bent and lifted Suzanne in his arms and smiled down at her, one of his rare smiles, looking so odd in that exhausted unshaved face. The agents were standing silently, watching them. Nobody made a move to stop him as he turned with her in his arms and walked out.

"Come love," he said, as he carried her over the doorstep, "let's go home."

THE END

Enjoy this excerpt from

Midnight Run

Midnight Book 2

The Warehouse's big steel fire doors closed behind them and suddenly the world fell silent. No music penetrated the door. All that was left of the clatter and chaos inside was a deep beat, more a vibration than a noise. It was exactly that time of night when it was too late for new customers to come to The Warehouse, and too early for the clients to be going home. They were alone in the large loading apron that now served as a parking lot.

It was snowing. Two feet from the door and they were in their own private, white world, pristine, silent and clean.

Claire's coat was a long cloak with a hood framing her face. She tipped her head up and closed her eyes in delight. She drew in a deep breath. The corners of her mouth curled up. "Oh," she breathed. "I love the snow." Her head turned and her eyes opened. "Thank you," she murmured. "For rescuing me and for offering to drive me home."

The hooded cloak, the dark night, the heartbreakingly beautiful young woman, the snow. It was harder than ever for Bud to shake off the feeling that he was caught in a fairy tale. The woodsman, maybe, escorting the Princess back to the palace after rescuing her from the dragon. Or the knight, coming to claim his fated bride.

She wasn't a Princess. He had to keep reminding himself of that. She was a perfectly ordinary Portland girl named Claire. Claire Schuyler. She spoke in a normal American accent and was wearing ordinary clothes. And yet, if she threw back her cloak to reveal a ball gown instead of a blue sweater dress and she'd said in a foreign accent that she was the Princess Esmeralda of a far-off kingdom, he wouldn't have been surprised.

"No need to thank me," he said and took her elbow. It had been really hard, back in The Warehouse, to keep his touch light as he guided her through the teeming pack of people. What he'd wanted to do—what he'd had to clench his teeth to keep from doing—was to lift her in his arms and carry her away. Find some quiet room somewhere and strip her clothes off. Find out if her skin was as soft as it looked, trace the shape of her breasts with his hands, pull out those sticks in her hair and watch it tumble over bare shoulders, curl around her breasts and hard little nipples.

His cock stirred in his pants.

Whoa.

This was definitely not what she'd want. Her rescuer coming on to her. She was taking a big chance, getting in a car with him, a total stranger. Granted, she didn't have much of a choice. The redheaded bitch had abandoned Claire outright, off to fuck the latest boy-friend. And the bartender was right—the taxis wouldn't come out here. No, she'd been stuck.

"Here we are," he said quietly, a hand on the passenger handle. The snow was falling in light drifts, big fat snowflakes, fairy tale snowflakes. Claire pushed her hood back and lifted her face to him, lips upturned. He found himself foolishly smiling back, though he wasn't much of a smiler. The flakes kissed her skin and melted at the warmth. He knew exactly how they felt.

He opened the passenger door and took in a deep breath. She was getting into a car with a man she didn't know. A man who outweighed her by at least 90 pounds and who was a foot taller than she was. Time to break the enchantment and tell her who he was.

Why was he hesitating? He'd be breaking cover, but he'd already done that with the bartender. That wasn't it.

Bud was used to being brutally honest with himself about himself and he knew the real reason he didn't want to say who he was.

Women had one of two reactions when they found out he was a homicide detective. They were either turned off or turned on. He didn't want either one from her. He didn't want her to shy away in disgust and he didn't want her to be morbidly curious about what it was like to fuck an armed man who investigates dead bodies for a living.

For a little while longer, he wanted her to be The Princess and he wanted to be her knight.

She was looking up at him as he hesitated in the vee of the open car door and he sighed. Time to break the spell.

"I want you to know you'll be safe with me," he said quietly. "I'm a—"

"I know," she interrupted, her voice just as quiet as his, as if both of them had been battered by the noise of The Warehouse. "I know I'm safe with you. I can feel it." Her eyes searched his for a long moment, luminous gorgeous blue eyes, full of trust. She smiled, bent and got into the passenger seat. He was left holding the door open, feeling like an idiot.

Okay.

He got in and started the engine, letting it warm up. They turned to each other and he had to grip the steering wheel hard not to pull her in his arms.

She was wearing some kind of light perfume that had been drowned out in the sharp smells of The Warehouse. Now the delicate scent all but reached out with insidious tendrils to grab hold of his brain and play havoc with the cells. The perfume, coupled with the stunning eyes and delicately uptilted mouth smiling at him, also made its way into his pants. He started getting a hard-on. Good thing his sheepskin jacket reached his knees.

This was crazy. He was crazy. He was going to escort her home, go back to his place, take a cold shower, fall into bed, then leave early tomorrow morning for Astoria where he'd fuck Nancy non-stop until Sunday night. Get the Princess out of his head.

"Okay." The engine was warm. "Where do I take you?"

She gave him the address. It was on the other side of the city, about eight blocks from his apartment complex. "I'm afraid I'm going to make you cross town," she apologized. "In the snow."

In the din of The Warehouse, when they'd had to shout to communicate, he hadn't had a chance to hear her speaking voice. It was just his damned luck that it was soft, light, feminine, seductive and sexy as hell.

Shit.

"No, that's okay." Bud pulled out of The Warehouse's parking lot. "I've got a lot of experience driving in the snow and I have snow tires. And chains, if necessary." He peered up out of the windshield at the fat, wet, lazy flakes. "This kind of snow won't stick to the ground anyway."

"It's so pretty, though," she said softly, smiling. She was looking out the window, as delighted as a child at Christmas.

"Mmm." Bud could hardly breathe. *She* was so pretty. So pretty it almost hurt. Her skin glowed like palest ivory in the lights from the dashboard. She was turned away from him, looking out the window and watching the snow so he could watch her—a much nicer view than the snow.

There was very little traffic but he was driving slowly so he could sneak frequent glances at her without running into a lamppost. She was in profile, a pale cameo against the dark window. Perfectly curved eyebrow, long lashes, straight nose with finely arched nostrils, the corner of her mouth uptilted in an unconscious smile. That must be her default expression. A smile.

She looked pretty and innocent and he shouldn't have this massive hard-on he'd developed. She wasn't his type at all.

He didn't like pretty and innocent. He liked women who knew what they were doing in bed and who knew what the score was.

He'd had a hard life and he had one of those jobs where you put on rubber boots and waded through the muck and filth of the worst humanity has to offer.

He'd seen it all—wife-beaters and hopheads and drunks. The lowest of the low. And the highest of the high. Respectable businessmen who hired a hit man to take out a business rival.

Society matrons who smothered their newborn children because the baby interfered with their social life. Rich youngsters who beat their parents to death because they wanted a bigger allowance.

Yeah, he'd seen it all. Twice. The last thing he needed was some innocent young miss who'd be stiff in bed and cling to him afterwards.

Nope, he was going to drive pretty little Miss Schuyler safely to her door, say goodnight politely like the gentleman he wasn't, go home, get some shuteye, then take off for his weekend of hot sex. Yup, that's what he'd do.

His cock wasn't listening to a word his head was saying.

His cock didn't give a shit about home or sleep. It didn't want Nancy Whosis, it wanted *her*, the Princess, and it wasn't taking no for an answer. He had a boner in his pants so hard he could knock on doors with it. She shifted a little in her seat and a little whiff of that perfume wafted his way and he nearly came in his pants.

Jesus, what was this? He hadn't come in his pants since he was 13 and Molly Everson took off her bra behind the Rexall. He'd always had a lot of sexual stamina and coming once had just primed the pump. Molly had left smiling. But that was a long time ago, a lot of women ago, and the Princess not only hadn't taken her bra off, she wasn't giving off any sex signals whatsoever.

Any other woman who wanted it would have had her hand on his thigh by now, would have been sighing and crossing her legs and giving him long meaningful glances. Pretending it was too hot in the car and unbuttoning. That's what Nancy had done two weeks ago when they'd taken a drive down the coast and she'd ended up giving him a blow job in the car.

Claire was just sitting there, a faint smile on her lips, watching the snow, buttoned up to the neck in her cloak, slim pretty hands still and folded in her lap. No come on at all.

But he remembered, and above all his cock remembered, how she'd filled the sweater dress she had on. She was slender, almost slight, but curvy with surprisingly full breasts. Round and full and high.

Walking behind her as they made their way around the Pit he'd had to clench his fists not to clasp her around her tiny waist. He had big hands and he'd bet he could almost span her waist. Hold her there as he kneed her legs apart from behind, slip right into her. She'd be tight, he'd bet anything on that. Tight and wet and...

Oh God. He nearly groaned aloud. This was torture. How much longer?

He tried to peer through the snow that was falling more thickly now and caught a glimpse of the white and blue street sign on the corner. Another three blocks to go and he could dump her on her doorstep and go home and jerk off. He was as hard as a rock. He wasn't going to let Nancy up for air this weekend, that's for sure. He felt like he could fuck for 48 hours straight.

But not Nancy.

Jesus, what had *that* thought come from? Since when was there a reasonably attractive woman—and Nancy was more than okay if a little on the clueless side—he couldn't fuck?

He needed to get rid of the Princess, right *now*, she was messing with his head.

He stepped on the gas a little and the wheels spun. The whole universe was conspiring against him, he thought, as he slowed the car back down. He could feel sweat breaking out. Come on, come on, let's get her home, hurry this *up*.

But the road was slippery and he was making lousy time.

"Turn to the right here," she said, scanning the street and even her voice in the dark turned him on. No, he was already turned on, the voice was just icing on the cake.

It was another tortuous ten minutes before he pulled up to a house that looked just like her—small, charming, nicely built and pretty. Jesus, this gentleman thing was deadly stuff because to keep in character he'd have to walk her to her door. With a hard-on. The knee-length coat would cover it but it was there and it fucking *hurt*.

He killed the engine, grimly determined to play the part of the gentleman to the bitter end, for the first and definitely the last time in his life. It would take two minutes, tops. Walk her up to her door, shake hands maybe, though just touching that smooth skin would be like lighting a detonator, then walk away—hobble away—with his hard-on. That's what he'd do.

"Here we are." His voice was hoarse. He cleared his throat. "I'll walk you—"

"Would you like to come in for some coffee?" she asked in a rush, the words tumbling over themselves. *Wouldyouliketocomeinforsomecoffee?* As if she'd been rehearsing it.

She'd turned to him fully, but wasn't meeting his eyes, asking his chin if he wanted to come in for coffee. Her breathing was slightly speeded up and the hand holding her cloak together was trembling. She was asking him in for more than coffee. She might not even be aware of it herself, but he was.

Coffee was a synonym for sex.

Absolutely not.

No sex, no. Not with her.

She was trouble with a capital T which rhymed with C which stood for Claire.

It wouldn't be happily vigorous sex for a couple of hours, then a handshake and goodbye, which was all he was looking for, all he wanted from a woman. He liked sex that was hard and long and uncomplicated. He didn't want sex with her. She had complication written all over that gorgeous face of hers. No sex with Claire Schuyler. No no no.

His head was clear on that and he opened his mouth to say no, but his cock got there first.

"Yeah, love to."

About the author:

Lisa Marie Rice is eternally 30 years old and will never age. She is tall and willowy and beautiful. Men drop at her feet like ripe pears. She has won every major book prize in the world. She is a black belt with advanced degrees in archeology, nuclear physics and Tibetan literature. She is a concert pianist. Did I mention the Nobel?Of course, Lisa Marie Rice is a virtual woman and exists only at the keyboard when writing erotic romance. She disappears when the monitor winks off.

Lisa Marie welcomes mail from readers. You can write to her c/o Ellora's Cave Publishing at 1337 Commerce Drive, Suite 13, Stow OH 44224.

Why an electronic book?

We live in the Information Age—an exciting time in the history of human civilization in which technology rules supreme and continues to progress in leaps and bounds every minute of every hour of every day. For a multitude of reasons, more and more avid literary fans are opting to purchase e-books instead of paperbacks. The question to those not yet initiated to the world of electronic reading is simply: *why?*

1. *Price.* An electronic title at Ellora's Cave Publishing runs anywhere from 40-75% less than the cover price of the exact same title in paperback format. Why? Cold mathematics. It is less expensive to publish an e-book than it is to publish a paperback, so the savings are passed along to the consumer.
2. *Space.* Running out of room to house your paperback books? That is one worry you will never have with electronic novels. For a low one-time cost, you can purchase a handheld computer designed specifically for e-reading purposes. Many e-readers are larger than the average handheld, giving you plenty of screen room. Better yet, hundreds of titles can be stored within your new library—a single microchip. (Please note that Ellora's Cave does not endorse any specific brands. You can check our website at www.ellorascave.com

for customer recommendations we make available to new consumers.)

3. *Mobility*. Because your new library now consists of only a microchip, your entire cache of books can be taken with you wherever you go.
4. *Personal preferences are accounted for*. Are the words you are currently reading too small? Too large? Too...**ANNOYING**? Paperback books cannot be modified according to personal preferences, but e-books can.
5. *Innovation*. The way you read a book is not the only advancement the Information Age has gifted the literary community with. There is also the factor of what you can read. Ellora's Cave Publishing will be introducing a new line of interactive titles that are available in e-book format only.
6. *Instant gratification*. Is it the middle of the night and all the bookstores are closed? Are you tired of waiting days—sometimes weeks—for online and offline bookstores to ship the novels you bought? Ellora's Cave Publishing sells instantaneous downloads 24 hours a day, 7 days a week, 365 days a year. Our e-book delivery system is 100% automated, meaning your order is filled as soon as you pay for it.

Those are a few of the top reasons why electronic novels are displacing paperbacks for many an avid reader. As always, Ellora's Cave Publishing welcomes your questions and comments. We invite you to email us at service@ellorascave.com or write to us directly at: 1337 Commerce Drive, Suite 13, Stow OH 44224.

ELLORA'S CAVE
ROMANTICA PUBLISHING